MW01087952

SHADOWSTRUT

A NIGHT WARDEN NOVEL

ORLANDO A. SANCHEZ

This is a work of fiction. All of the characters, organizations, and events portrayed in this novel are either products of the authors' imagination or are used fictitiously and are not to be construed as real. Any resemblance to actual events, locales, organizations, or persons, living or dead, is entirely coincidental.

© 2019 Orlando A. Sanchez

All rights reserved, including the right to reproduce this book, or portions thereof, in any form.

Published by: Bitten Peaches Publishing

Cover Art: Gene Mollica Studios www.genemollica.com

Sometimes fear of the dark can keep you alive.

Grey and Koda have a lead on the supplier of Redrum X—a new strain of the deadly drug that creates UV resistant vampires. Preventing the streets of New York City from being flooded with the mindless creatures was only the first step.

Each night as darkness falls, body counts rise. Someone or something has made nights in the city... fatal. Grey must find who or what is doing the killing and stop them. He only has one clue. Rumors of a Mr. Dark are being whispered in the streets.

Is this Mr. Dark responsible for the deaths? Now together with Koda, Grey will enter a world no Night Warden has encountered. A world of darkness no one has escaped.

Can a dark mage wielding a darker blade bring light to save others?

ONE

*The night for one of the night, the day for
one of the day*

— —BASQUE PROVERB

*Maybe you have to know the darkness
before you can appreciate the light.*

— —MADELEINE L'ENGLE

"He said he wasn't scared, never scared of the dark." Street looked down at the broken body. "That was the last time we spoke, then this."

The arms and legs were bent at unnatural angles. Pieces of bone protruded through his clothing. It reminded me of a child breaking a doll, except the doll was a young mage. Someone-or something-angry did this. I looked past the brokenness and blood. Life made us all a little broken and bloody. What made me pause was the face. Whatever this mage faced in his last moments, it had scared him out of his mind.

This mage had died terrified, and it had been painful.

Sweet bitterness filled my mouth. It was like biting down on a lemon and chasing it with a spoonful of honey. Ambient magic caused my taste buds to fire...one of the side effects of my condition. Every death was different. The sweetness in this one meant serious power had been unleashed.

Street was jumpier than usual, a bad sign. A jumpy mage of his power, with no recollection of his abilities, meant dead bodies. First thing I needed to do was get him calm.

"How about we go to The Dive and get some food inside you?" I asked. "When was the last time you ate?"

"Ate...ate?" Street looked around, his eyes darting in every direction. I could feel the energy coming off him in waves. "Can't think of food. Look...look!"

"How about some place closer?" Koda asked, looking at Street's face. Her eyes gave off a faint red glow as she glanced at the body of the dead mage. "We may want to get him away from the body, Grey. It seems to be bothering him."

Koda, a Night Warden in training, had joined me when Hades had informed me of her imminent retirement. She had worked for him as a cleaner, an assassin, who had botched a job. Corbel, the Hound of Hades, had to step in and fix the error, but that was enough for Hades. She either worked with me, or stopped breathing...permanently. I preferred working alone, but I wasn't going to let Hades ghost her, even though she was a headache of epic proportions.

She had modified her look since she had started

working with me. Her long, cascading black hair had lost some of the red streaks. These days, she kept it in a long braid, tipped with iron ornaments. Her pale, translucent skin was covered by wordweaver leathers with similar properties to my duster.

In addition to being an intense migraine, Koda possessed abilities that made her dangerous. She was a runic cipher. Ciphers were considered nil, nothing, both figuratively and literally. In a different age, when no energy signature could be found, ciphers were killed at birth. These days, the magical community would shun and ostracize her, but they would fall just short of trying to eliminate her… overtly, of course.

Aside from her weapons, Koda had no energy signature whatsoever. She was a runic ghost. This made her rare and targeted. Hades knew this and had probably felt my life wasn't exciting enough when he'd 'suggested' I take her on and train her as a Night Warden.

"Let's get this place sealed off," I said. "I want to know who, or what, did this."

A hint of cinnamon lingered in the air. I looked around to see where it may be coming from, but I saw nothing.

"Are you going to check now?" Koda said, pulling out caution tape. "It's going to attract attention."

"Can't be helped," I said. "Once the authorities get on the scene, they'll taint the area with too many energy signatures."

"How many homeless mages are there?"

"More than anyone wants to admit," I said, keeping the anger in check. "Cast-offs, ostracized by their sects or banned. Use the wrong spell and no one is clapping."

"Is that what happened to you?"

"People try to kill what they don't understand."

"Mages too?" Koda asked, surprised. "Wouldn't they be more—?"

"*Especially* the magical community," I growled, remembering the Night Wardens after Jade. "The nail that sticks out gets hammered down...and then crushed."

"And these homeless mages?"

"Crushed and beaten nails." The anger gripped me. I took a long breath and unclenched my jaw. "If that wasn't bad enough, now someone—"

"Or something," Koda added.

"Or *something*," I conceded, "is using them for target practice."

"Who speaks for the voiceless?" Koda asked quietly. "This is bad."

"I do—*we* do," I said, my voice hard. "That's what it means to be a Night Warden. When everyone says no and washes their hands, we're in the thick of it. Now, move out of the way so I can do this."

"Fine," Koda said with a shudder. "Let me get Street out of the park before you start. You know how he gets when you do that sword thing."

I nodded as Koda left the area with Street.

I looked around the park. Nightfall usually emptied it of all except the most brave...or foolish. Word of this attack would get out, and the NYTF would get here eventually, but it wouldn't be a priority. In a city this size, this death was one of hundreds today. By the time the NYTF arrived on this scene, I'd be gone.

I extended my arm and formed my sword, *kokoro kokutan no ken,* which translated loosely to Darkspirit. The sword was special because, aside from being a dark blade holding the sentient manifestation of Izanami—the goddess of creation

4

and destruction, it was the only thing keeping me alive these days. Its black blade glistened in the low light as the red runes along its length pulsed with energy. Black tendrils enveloped me as the sword absorbed the remaining light around it.

I buried the point of the sword into the ground next to the corpse and then I stepped back. Tendrils of energy flowed around the body of the recently deceased mage. The bitterness in my mouth increased, and I spat to one side.

"What are you getting?" I asked. "He doesn't look like a rummer."

A few years back, in the pursuit of power, I, together with several other Night Wardens, had unleashed a forbidden spell—an entropic dissolution. The spell had become unstable, killed my partner Jade, and proceeded to do the same to me...just slowly. I managed to get the spell under control, but not before the damage was done. I had made peace with the idea of dying, until a conversation with Hades changed that.

'A dark blade for a dark mage.' Those were his exact words. *'This sword can keep you alive.'* I didn't believe him initially, and by the time I did, it was too late. Darkspirit and I had bonded. He gave me the sword, and then suggested I locate the source of the tainted Redrum being unleashed in my city. Like I'd ever had a choice.

I was in the middle of pursuing a lead when Street had called me about this dead mage. At first, I thought it was another rummer who had burned out from too much of the drug, but this was different. The broken body lying on the ground in front of me was no rummer.

<This is old magic, mage.>

"I'm getting that," I said into the night. Izanami

could communicate directly into my brain. I refused to answer her the same way, even though I probably could. Call me old-fashioned. "Can you trace it? Who or what could cast this spell? Was it a pavormancer?"

<This is deeper than pavormancy—older, more primal.>

"Older than pavormancy?" I asked. "Any idea what it could be? 'Older than pavormancy' is a little on the vague side."

<I cannot ascertain its origin from a corpse. If you place me in his blood, perhaps I can...>

"That's going to be a no on the blood-dipping."

Izanami was constantly looking for opportunities to get extra doses of blood. Damn sword needed to belong to a vampire, not a dark mage.

<Then you will have to resort to actual study.>

"Shit," I said, reabsorbing Darkspirit. "That means homework, but we can't leave the body like this."

I cast two spells. First, a spatial displacement spell. This would make it impossible for anyone to accidentally 'discover' the body. The second was more complicated: a temporal regression spell. It allowed me to take a sample of the corpse under the influence of what had killed him. The time component alone was promising to split my skull with a world-class headache. I gritted my teeth and cast.

Before my bond with Izanami, this cast would've been excruciating. After the bond, it was a dull, throbbing, ice pick of pain from the oncoming migraine. The bond didn't remove the pain entirely, my condition was too far advanced for that, but it did mitigate the worst of the symptoms and stopped me from dying, but no one said I would be pain-free.

I patched into the NYTF through my communicator.

"Ramirez," I said, and waited. A few seconds later, the gruff voice of Director Ramirez of the NYTF came on the line.

The New York Task Force, or NYTF, was a quasi-military police force, created to deal with any supernatural event occurring in New York City. They were paid to deal with the things that couldn't be explained to the general public without causing mass hysteria.

They were led by Angel Ramirez, who was one of the best directors the NYTF had ever had. After a certain Agency started doing business in the city, our friendship had grown strained due to the constant destruction. I promised him I would have a conversation with the demolition duo soon.

"Grey," Ramirez said, sounding tired. "Where's the body?"

"How did you know I wasn't just calling to invite you to The Dive?"

"Simple. When Simon, his devil-dog, and the Brit are involved, I get calls about the buildings in my city exploding. It's usually a landmark or something historic, difficult or impossible to replace. I swear those two must hate me."

"And me?"

"Bodies…plenty of bodies," Ramirez answered, his voice grim. "Now, tell me where so I can have my guys pick it up."

"The park, near the lake in the trees, just west of the Bethesda Fountain."

"Did you do one of your spatial things where no one can see it?"

"Yes, look for the caution tape."

"Another rummer?" Ramirez asked. "I hate those."

"No, this is something else," I said. "If you hear anything out of the ordinary, let me know."

"Out of the ordinary? In this city? You must be joking. Everything is out of the ordinary."

"I meant more than the usual," I said. "Street found the body."

"Shit," Ramirez answered. "How is he? And, more importantly, *where* is he?"

"I'm going to drop him off at Haven for a few days, at least until he calms down."

"Thank you," he said with a sigh. "He'll be safer out of the park."

"So will we."

"Do you have any leads?"

"One, but it's thin," I said. "I'll let you know what I find."

Something older than pavormancy meant I had to go visit the largest magical library in the city.

I needed to pay Aria a visit at the Cloisters.

TWO

"**K**oda, we need to drop Street off at Haven and then head uptown to Aria."

"Got it," she answered, heading up the stairs. "Meet you at the Beast. My bike is close."

The Beast was my mode of transportation. Some felt she was evil, but I knew differently. Killing three drivers doesn't make a car evil, just cursed. Her body was based on a SuNaTran modified 1970 Chevy Camaro. Like the Phantoms they provided, the Beast was equipped with armor plating where it mattered. Cecil, the owner of SuNaTran, initially tried to paint her Byzantium. It didn't take—the paint burned right off, and left the exterior matte black. It might not be evil, but she had taste. The Beast could never be purple, no matter how fancy you dressed up the color.

I took a moment to admire the fountain. The Terrace had come a long way from the place to get your drugs in the seventies. Now, it was a tourist attraction —and a final resting place for the mage I'd just found. Temperance, Purity, Health, and Peace weren't in attendance tonight. No angel was going to descend upon the waters and bring that broken mage back. I

9

was sliding headfirst into a morose mood, and shook myself loose from the gloom that filled my thoughts.

Some ghosts never leave. No matter how hard you try, they cling to you, like blood that can never be washed off. God, now I was going positively Shakespearean. I needed to get the hell out of the park.

I had left the Beast on Terrace Drive, near the entrance to Bethesda Terrace. I'd have to head downtown on the east side of the city to drop Street off at Haven, and then shoot uptown to Aria. I let my senses expand as I crossed the pink stone surrounding Bethesda Fountain, and felt...nothing. This area of the park was usually empty at this time of night, but not devoid of ambient signatures.

Something was wrong.

The first thing I felt was the undercurrent of fear, which lasted all of half a second. The fear tried to embrace me but found nothing to latch on to. I had faced and made peace with all of my fears long ago.

I'd had my partner—the woman I loved—die in my arms. I'd seen my closest friends perish, or become drug-addicted, mindless creatures of the night. I had faced death and embraced it, and still did...every day. There was nothing left for me to fear.

Something was approaching, and the first play was to get me scared. Epic fail.

"You don't feel fear?" a voice said in the night. "How curious."

"Sorry to disappoint," I said, facing the fountain. The acoustics of the Terrace made it hard to pinpoint where the voice came from. "That your work?"

I pointed to where the broken mage lay.

"How do you not feel fear?" the voice asked again. "Everyone feels fear of some kind."

"Fear and I have an understanding," I said, opening my duster, giving me access to my gun, Fatebringer. I'd had to have Aria recreate it after Lyrra, the former head of the Night Wardens, decided the first one was better in pieces. Remaking it had been a project of epic proportions. The rune work alone taking several days. Aria had used some choice curses…most of them directed my way. Between Fatebringer and the leathers for Koda, I'd owe Aria for the rest of my life.

"What kind of understanding?"

"You didn't answer my question," I said. "Did you kill the mage?"

"One of mine facilitated the end of the mage."

I wish I knew what the hell that meant.

"One of yours?" I let my hand drift over to Fatebringer. My senses still read that I was alone in the Terrace. "Who are you, again?"

I didn't materialize Darkspirit, because I had a feeling that the moment I did…all bets would be off. Whatever this was, it was testing the waters.

"You know me, mage."

"No, can't say that I do," I said, backing up. I was getting a distinct 'time to vacate the premises' vibe. "I'd remember a disembodied voice trying to scare me."

Bitterness filled my mouth. The same bitterness I'd sensed near the broken mage, but with no aftertaste of honey. Serious dark magic. The level of power around me began increasing. Slowly at first, then exponentially. Whatever I was facing was rapidly approaching 'out of my league' in power. A bass rumble echoed around me, removing all doubt about the level of power I was facing.

"You…KNOW ME."

The words reverberated around the Terrace, and I stopped backing up. I wasn't alone any longer.

"Saying it louder doesn't mean it's clearer… Oh, shit." I began to sense more energy signatures. "What did you say your name was?"

Laughter echoed around the park. "You will learn it soon enough, if you survive."

"That sounds very glass-half-empty."

No response.

I sensed them all around me, and realized this was what must have happened to the mage. The smell of strong coffee mixed with something foul filled my lungs. Powerful magic leaning hard on the dark side.

Rummers had entered the Terrace, and they weren't here for a chat.

Whatever the voice was, it had the ability to mask an entire area. The rummers closing in on my position were reading slightly off. I could sense the influence of the Redrum, but there was something else, something…dark.

These rummers were being controlled by the power I was sensing around me.

THREE

Redrum destroyed most of the brain, turning the rummers into little more than ravenous animals who were incapable of speech. The creatures closing in on my position weren't going to be swayed by words—pleading or begging.

Not that I was going to attempt any un-bladed conversation.

I had loaded Fatebringer with LITE rounds—Light Irradiated Tungsten Entropy rounds. They were perfect rummer erasers for garden-variety rummers, and after my last run-in with ogres, that little dash of entropy covered my ass against anything—rummer or more.

Tessa, the proprietor of the Moving Market, wouldn't sell me LITE ammunition, not because she didn't want to, but because she couldn't. No one could. My rounds were not available in stores. You couldn't buy LITE rounds anywhere, especially not in the Moving Market. I had created the LITE rounds. They were dangerous, lethal, highly unstable, and probably frowned upon by any of the governing bodies operating in the city.

Rummers may be the size of average humans, but

that didn't mean they were harmless. They were faster, stronger, and more resilient than normals. Redrum gave them heightened senses, night vision, enhanced hearing, and an insane sense of smell. A mindless, deadly package. They only had one major flaw I could exploit, which was that a few seconds of concentrated UV radiation led to an explosive messy end.

Enter, LITE rounds.

Without the entropy, LIT rounds were making the new and improved rummers laugh. Somehow, the new strain of Redrum was giving them immunity to LIT ammunition, taking three or four rounds to end them. Some of the rummers had even been spotted during the day not spontaneously bursting into piles of ash. This was the nightmare Lyrra wanted to unleash on the city—super UV-resistant rummers. I thought I had caught it in time.

I was wrong.

Now I was facing, what...dark, UV-resistant rummers? This insanity was getting out of hand.

I materialized Darkspirit again.

<Have you brought me out to feed, or to give you information as you stick me in the ground?>

"We have a situation."

I let my senses expand, and I felt the approaching rummers. There were easily six to ten of them. It was hard to get a reading because of the throbbing in my head, and because of their diffused energy signature. They read as one large group, but it was hard to break them down into individual threats.

<Their blood is tainted.>

"You're being picky...now?"

<I'm merely stating a fact.>

"I could always use Fatebringer. *It* won't give me attitude."

14

<Use your gun?>

"Yes. It happens to fire when I pull the trigger and, remarkably, has nothing to say about my targets."

<There are too many of them. You would be overrun, die a painful—if not deserved—death, and then that would force me to find a new host.... No thank you.>

Izanami was probably right. I was sensing more than ten as the rummers got closer.

"I'm glad my welfare and safety are such a priority to you."

<They are. It took me considerable time to find you. I would prefer to avoid the search for a new host.>

"Would hate to inconvenience you."

<It wasn't easy, you know. You would think a vampire would wield me often enough to sate my thirst.>

"Imagine that...a vampire opting not to use you. I suppose it wouldn't have anything to do with the fact that no vampire is strong enough to wield you without turning to ash?"

<Nothing ventured, nothing gained. Their fear was distasteful.>

The rummers were approaching slowly. They must have sensed Darkspirit, which wasn't surprising. She gave off a decidedly dark vibe that whispered 'get closer, so I can eat you.'

"I'll do the wielding and you do the cutting—that's how this works, last time I checked."

<You haven't forgotten what I am, have you, mage?>

"Besides a colossal pain in my ass?"

<Your attempts at humor are wasted. It is a poor coping mechanism.>

"Works for me. If you have a point, get to it. These rummers don't look like the patient type. Only thing keeping them away right now is your welcoming presence."

<I am what I am and have accepted that. You would do well to do the same.>

"We can have a heart-to-blade later…spit it out."

<I am a siphon. Whatever I rend or undo is siphoned into the one bonded to me.>

Shit.

I was still getting used to this whole 'being bonded to a blood-thirsty blade' situation. What she'd just described sounded unpleasant…especially when rummers were involved.

<You may wield. I will cut, but you will receive, mage.>

This was getting worse by the second. I cast a spell. The dull throbbing spiked into the stratosphere for a second, and then it calmed down.

"You may be a siphon, but that doesn't mean I have to take what you're giving."

<That…is an elegantly lethal solution.>

"I'd like to think so."

<I doubt it will be effective.>

"Let's find out," I said as the first rummer lunged at me.

FOUR

I was never big on blades.

I could use them, every Night Warden could, but it wasn't my preferred method of fighting.

Edged weapons required the user to get close. For most of the creatures I dealt with, distance was my friend. No one wanted to dance with an angry ogre, or a mob of rummers if you can take them down from a distance instead.

Besides, rummers smelled like hell. Their bodies were decomposing, only kept intact by the effects of the Redrum and the turning. The last thing I needed, or wanted, was a lungful of eau de putrescence. I'd rather take a tour of the New York City sewers without a breathing apparatus.

The spell I cast shunted the energy Darkspirit absorbed back into the blade, making it a repository, of sorts. I had a feeling Izanami just didn't want to hold on to tainted rummer energy.

"What the hell is taking so long, old man?" Koda's voice came over my comms. "You get lost down there?"

I slid to the side and slashed horizontally, bisecting the rummer at the waist. It burst into dust.

That wasn't odd. Rummers usually disintegrated when hit by LITE rounds or a blade like Darkspirit.

What was odd was that only one rummer attacked. They usually moved in swarms and attacked as a group, using superior numbers to overwhelm their targets.

These rummers were acting peculiar. It was almost as if they were studying me, looking for a weakness to exploit. Whatever was in the darkness could mask their presence and control their default behavior.

"Stay over there and keep Street away from the park," I said quickly. "I got rummers here, and they're acting strange."

"What do you mean, strange?"

"It's hard to describe…they're waiting."

"Waiting?" Koda asked. "What do you mean 'they're waiting'? Waiting for what?"

"Exactly," I said. "Stay out of the park and keep Street back."

"Rummers aren't the only ones acting strange tonight."

"If I need help, which I won't, I'll let you know."

"I'm taking Street to Haven," she answered. "He's getting agitated, and the last thing I need is a powerful but unstable mage losing it while I stand at ground zero. Oh, and Street should be safe too."

"Hilarious," I said. "If I need an assist, I'll—"

"Squeal like a little girl?" she asked. "I'm sorry… growl like a fearsome Night Warden?"

"You should be gone."

"Already a memory, see you downtown."

"Good," I said with a growl. "Wait for me at Haven. When you get there, have Roxanne see Street. Don't let anyone else near him, he won't react well.

Call her when you're close. I'll get there as soon as I can, but it feels like it's going to be a long night."

I heard the roar of the Shroud.

The Shroud was a SuNaTran—Supernatural Transport—variant of the Ecosse superbike, outfitted with extras, like camouflage and biometric locks. I'd had Cecil reconfigure the security measures to accept Koda's lack of a signature. He'd managed to have it read her absence of a signature as a signature. How he did it still mildly melted my brain. He'd somehow extrapolated Ziller's theorem of negation, and applied runes to the bike that could pick up on Koda. He tried explaining it to me, but I had to stop him after a few sentences—and I'm a mage.

"Don't get dead," Koda said. I heard her taking off into the night and removing Street from the madness that waited in the park.

Even though I'd used Darkspirit to end the first rummer, I felt no rush of energy. As ineffective as the spell I cast was, it must have been working, or Izanami was filtering the energy on her own.

"You can't control them forever," I said into the night.

"I don't need forever, Warden," the voice answered. "I only need long enough to see you torn to shreds."

It knew I was a Night Warden, which was enough to get me thinking about what this entity was. I had an idea, but I'd need to go see Honor, the head of the Central Archive and proprietor of the Dragonflies on the Reeds, to get more information...if I survived tonight.

"Oh, hey, welcome back," I said, releasing energy into my duster and biting back the pain that rushed down my neck. "You never did tell me your name.

I've never met a shy creature of evil. Or were you given a horrible name? Fluffy the Fear-Caster?"

"You dare to mock me?" the voice answered. "I will make sure your death is agonizingly slow."

Magic-types, for all the power they wielded, had unnaturally delicate egos. A little button-pushing was usually enough to get them riled up. I liked to start with names, because names have power.

"Ahh, Fluffy, did I hit a nerve?" I asked, feeling the magic course through my coat. "No need to be sensitive. I mean, my name is Grey Stryder. I sound like a horrible knock-off sneaker."

"Kill him."

I sensed the rummers suddenly kick into high gear. They weren't waiting anymore.

"Let the shredding begin."

FIVE

My duster was no ordinary coat.

Contrary to popular opinion, I didn't get it for the 'look.' I do admit, it gave me a certain air of extraordinary badassery, which I normally didn't possess. Like a certain notorious magic-user in the Midwest who runs around with fae these days, my coat was purely functional, not cosmetic.

It served as my first, and usually last, line of defense. Even though it was slightly worn, it was a gift from Aria of the Wordweavers, one of the most powerful runecasters on the face of the Earth. It was the only one of its kind, and it had saved my ass more times than I could remember.

It was like getting that favorite sweater from a distant aunt. If I didn't wear it, she'd ask why and then proceed to make me a new one. There was no getting around it. I was wearing a duster whether I wanted to or not...all year round.

Aria had imbued it with several runes of immense power, weaving in special properties for the dragonfly emblem. The pockets were dimensional locations, making time and relative distance in space a theoretical construct, allowing me to carry everything I needed and more. Basically, it was bigger on the inside than on the outside.

I didn't think it was possible, but in all my years as a mage, I had never seen anything like it. Aria had achieved runic overkill. I wondered what she thought I faced every night on the city streets. Even though it looked like worn leather, the runes made it stronger than Kevlar and Dragonscale combined.

Considering I wasn't bulletproof, magic-proof, or immune to large bursts of flame, using it as a shield had come in handy. Aria knew my limitations around casting, which meant the constant defensive spells the duster used were passive, not requiring active participation.

I avoided most of the bells and whistles because they required high-powered spells to activate, which meant high-powered pain for me. Due to the attention of ogres, rummers, and other creatures of the night, it was starting to look a bit ragged around the edges. I preferred to think of it as not-so-gently broken in. I'd have Aria do some work on it when I saw her next…if I saw her again.

As the rummers closed in, I spoke the words of power that activated the coat. The sensation of liquid lava burned through my chest as my muscles seized. The duster went from dark brown leather, to black with a metallic sheen. The dragonfly emblem on the rear glowed a deep violet, with black and red accents coruscating over its surface. I gritted my teeth against the pain, and enclosed myself in the coat.

<You intend to face them all?>

"Don't see much of a choice…do you?"

<You could run away. Since you refuse to take their siphoned power.>

"The first lesson you learn as a Night Warden, always stack the odds in your favor." I moved back. "Never fight fair, because fair doesn't exist. Misdirect and attack from strength when you appear weak."

<Those are wonderful platitudes. Were they created by a Night Warden surrounded by blood-thirsty vampires intent on killing their target and draining him dry?>

"Somehow, I doubt that," I said, gesturing as the rummers came closer. "Fighting for your life doesn't lend itself to pithy comments in the heat of battle."

<Unless you're an old, dying, Night Warden with delusions of grandeur.>

"I'm not old…yet."

I gestured, and black tendrils shot out from Darkspirit, impaling several rummers and destroying them.

<Using their own energy against them? Clever. You're more intelligent than your actions would indicate.>

"It's called recycling," I said, catching my breath. "Thank you, I think."

The smell of old coffee joined with a low-pitched rumble filled my senses.

A scream cut through the park, as the rummers pounced. Behind the scream, I heard the low laughter of the creature controlling them.

The first two came at once. I drew Fatebringer and fired, punching holes in one, and then thrust forward, burying Darkspirit in the other. Both burst into dust. Sometimes it didn't pay to be first.

I rotated around a slash, letting my duster take the impact. I introduced the rummer to Darkspirit, as I parried another lunge of claws. More dust.

Another scream behind me. I stabbed to the rear and fired forward, ending two more.

Screaming on a sneak attack? Not very sneaky.

23

"You will die, Warden," the voice said. "You will embrace me."

"I *will* die," I said, cutting through two more rummers and ending them, "just not today."

The smell of burning wood filled the area, followed by the resonating foghorn of doom, as I called it. The taste of old, rancid lemon flooded my mouth, and I spat to one side. This was serious, dark, powerful magic.

"What the hell?" I muttered, as I sensed the signature of something big and nasty. "Is that you, Fluffy?"

More laughter. I was seriously beginning to question Fluffy's sense of humor. I started backing out of the Terrace. Even the remaining rummers had run away from whatever was incoming. When rummers run, that was my cue to get gone.

"I was saving this for later," the voice said, "but it seems you are ready to die now."

"You know," I said, absorbing Darkspirit and moving faster up the stairs, "I appreciate the sentiment, but you didn't need to go through all that trouble...really."

Whatever it was read like an industrial-sized rummer. I wasn't in a hurry for a meet-and-greet.

A roar filled the Terrace as trees were uprooted and crushed. I looked in the direction of the destruction, and my brain momentarily seized. I was looking at a rummer but one that was the size of an ogre. One of the rummers apparently hadn't gotten the 'get scarce' memo. The enormous rummogre reached out and snatched up the clueless rummer and bit off its head, casting the body aside. What was left burst to dust midair.

"Fuck me," I hissed, as the foghorn reached Inception-levels of volume. I stopped climbing the steps, realizing I was going to have to put this thing down. "What the fuck, Fluffy?"

"You *will* die...tonight," Fluffy answered, as more laughter filled the park. "Goodbye, Warden."

This was going to suck.

SIX

The park became still as the rummogre scanned the Terrace.

It was a giant, man-shaped creature. Scars covered its muscular body. Its disfigured and twisted face put the 'horror' in horrible. Ogres, on their own, were creatures to be avoided. They were dangerous, deadly, and stank like garbage covered in feces, then drenched in dog vomit…on a good day.

This hybrid monstrosity shared an aroma of maximum stench, that wrapped itself around me, punched me mercilessly in the face a few times, stomped on my lungs, and brought tears to my eyes.

"What the holy hell?" I asked, breathing shallowly to avoid suffocation. "The city's going to need to nuke this area to get rid of that odor."

I let my senses expand, and I realized I was alone in the park, except for the gigantic rummogre looking for its next meal. Frankly, I was insulted. The least Fluffy could've done was stick around to see if this thing erased me.

It was plain rude, but informative. Could Fluffy not hang about for long? Did he have a curfew? So many questions. I doubted the rummogre had answers for me.

I focused on the creature and took a deep breath, against my better judgment, letting it out slowly. Fatebringer even with LITE rounds, would—at best —tickle this thing. There were a few spells I could cast. All of them would leave me catatonic for days, not to mention bring every magical governing body to my doorstep for a chat.

Using Darkspirit openly in the city was enough to make some of them nervous. Casting dark spells of undoing would push them past nervous into angry elimination-mode. I wasn't quite ready to take on the Council.

We had an understanding. They left me alone, and I didn't bring their world crashing down around them in an angry fit of cataclysmic, dark mageness. So far, it was working. We just traded dirty looks and insults whenever our paths crossed.

Not surprisingly, not one member of the Dark Council happened to be roaming the rummer-infested park this evening. It was amazing how they always managed to be busy when these things occurred. I formed Darkspirit, and headed down the stairs towards the monster.

<You're walking toward that beast?>

"Your powers of observation are off the charts, Izzy."

<I've warned you not to call me that.>

She hated the nickname. Which was why I used it.

"We have to stop that thing," I said. "Fluffy created it, and we have to undo it. Can you handle it?"

<The question is, can you? And who is Fluffy?>

"I'll explain later," I said, whispering ancient words under my breath. The pain ratcheted up

28

slowly, gripped me by the base of the neck, and hovered around anesthesia-free root-canal level.

<Are you sure you can face this creature?>

It was the right question. The only way to deal with the rummogre was to give Darkspirit free reign, unleashing its power. It wasn't as bad as casting dark spells of world-ending destruction, but it would raise some eyebrows, especially among the resident mages.

And it would hurt.

This kind of magic didn't do subtle well. I looked around, and noticed zero of those mages in my immediate vicinity, which was exactly how many fucks I possessed to give, if they got their panties in a bunch.

The rummogre turned and narrowed its eyes, noticing me. Its movements weren't the erratic, random jerks of the smaller rummers. This thing was moving slowly, methodically, with purpose. Its eyes held intelligence, and that intelligence was hungry.

"I'm going to eat you, little wizard," it said, its gravelly voice carrying throughout the Terrace. Part of my brain was still contemplating the 'run to the Beast, and drive away' option. "Right after I rip off your arms and legs."

I had to remember to give Fluffy an extra stab for this evening's entertainment.

"That's just uncalled for," I said, holding my ground as it thumped its way to me. "Dark mages will give you indigestion, so you don't want to eat me. I'm sure a light mage will be along at some point. He'd be much tastier than me."

I unleashed Darkspirit.

Black tendrils of energy erupted from a muffled explosion of dark energy.

<Yes, mage. Finally you understand what must be done.>

29

ORLANDO A. SANCHEZ

The tendrils felt alive, and I realized these were extensions of the runic filaments that connected me to my psycho sword.

"I'm going to kill you," the rummogre said with a growl, pounding the ground with a massive fist.

My body screamed as the pain gripped me. The rational part of my brain shook its head, packed its bags, and walked away, waving. That left the primal, feral, and pissed-off part of me.

I smiled as the rummogre closed.

"You first," I said as I ran at the monster.

SEVEN

Ogres were slow-moving freight trains of violence.

Rummogres were not slow. In fact, they were surprisingly fast. This lesson came to me courtesy of the huge, fast-moving fist that launched me into a nearby wall, cracking the brick.

My duster absorbed and dampened most of the blow, which meant my spine remained intact, allowing me to roll away from the second blow that cratered the same wall.

Black tendrils shot forward from Darkspirit, burying themselves in the rummogre's body. I didn't bother with Fatebringer, and went in with the cutting immediately. I stepped inside its stance and slashed down behind the knee.

It screamed in anger and agony, burying an elbow in my side with a fantastic precision that my ribs didn't appreciate. I slid back several feet from the blow.

I gestured, forming an orb of black energy. It crackled with excess power radiating around it. I caught my breath, and released the orb as my vision went slightly out of focus.

ORLANDO A. SANCHEZ

"Fuck," I muttered under my breath. "Not now. Please, not now."

It lunged for me, attempting a bear hug that would have ended my days of walking upright, or walking...period.

I slashed across its arms as the orb impacted its chest. It looked down to where the orb had hit, and then back up at me. A sick, malicious smile spread across its lips.

"Looks like the wizard has run out of power," it said.

"I'm not taking it personally, but not everyone who uses magic is a wizard, you know," I corrected. "There are some very accomplished mages in this city."

"Mage or wizard," it said with a growl, "your little spells can't hurt me."

"I'm not looking to hurt you," I said with a gasp, as the pain decided this was a good time to introduce itself anew. "I'm looking to end you."

I threw Darkspirit. The rummogre caught it with a grin.

"And now you've given me your weapon," the rummogre said with a laugh. The intelligence exhibited by this monster was disturbing. "You're not very good at this, are you?"

I whispered, and Darkspirit reverted to black mist, surrounding the creature. The rummogre looked around, surprised.

"I didn't give *it* to you," I said with a final gesture. "I gave *you* to it."

The mist swirled around the rummogre, as black tendrils erupted from its body. The orb that had hit it earlier exploded outward. The black mist was actually composed of small blades that cut through the air...and the rummogre.

32

I staggered back to the steps, and fell to one knee as the rummogre's screams filled the night. In seconds, it was gone. I outstretched a hand, and Darkspirit flowed back into my body.

"If you feed me that tainted energy," I said, gritting my teeth against the pain of casting, "I'll make sure your next residence is a glass case in some dusty museum no one ever visits."

<I have no intention of feeding you anything. I require energy to sustain my form as well. That creature sufficed... for now.>

"Glad I could provide you with a meal," I said, making my way to the Beast. "Whoever or whatever made that thing is still out there. I need help."

<Besides me?>

"Yes, besides you," I snapped. "Not everything is solved by cutting it down to small, unrecognizable pieces."

<Really? It has been my experience that is exactly the best way to solve problems.>

EIGHT

I placed my hand on the Beast, and it unlocked with a metallic clang. An orange wave of energy raced across its chassis. I opened the heavy door, stumbled inside, and sat in the driver's seat for a few seconds, gathering my breath.

Who or what could create a rummogre? I needed answers, but first I had to make sure Street was safe.

I made the call to Haven.

"Director DeMarco," Roxanne said after two rings.

"Hey, Rox," I said with a grunt, as I placed my hand on the dashboard panel, starting the Beast with a roar of the engine. "How's Street?"

"Was that you I sensed earlier, Grey?"

"What are you talking about?" I feigned innocence. "Earlier when?"

Roxanne DeMarco was the director of Haven, one of the largest medical facilities in the city. They treated both normals and supernaturals, and they contained the strongest supernatural detention area on the Eastern seaboard.

Aside from being an excellent director, Rox was also one of the most powerful sorceresses I knew.

Getting on her bad side usually meant I spent a few days 'under observation' in one of her null rooms.

Considering where I was, the fact that she could sense my activity meant I was going to get calls from other not-so-friendly mages in the near future.

"You can't lie to save your life," Rox answered. "Don't bother denying it. You act like I wouldn't know your signature. Besides, your apprentice told me where you were. Two plus two equals one stubborn Night Warden."

Shit, I should've remembered Koda would tell her about the park. I was so focused on Street, I'd completely forgotten.

"She's not an apprentice," I said. "Is Street okay?"

"He'll be fine," Rox said with a sigh. "He's jumpier than usual. What was out there, Grey?"

"I don't know," I said, driving out of the park. "There were plenty of rummers, but there was something else—something that controlled them."

"Controlled them?" she asked, and I could hear the concern. "How is that possible? Once they turn, they're mindless beasts with only one urge…to feed."

"That's what I thought," I said, leaving out the rummogre. "Seems I was wrong. Can you ask Mr. Tea & Crumpets if he's picked up on anything odd in the city lately?"

"His name is Tristan, and I guess I can ask," she said, sighing deeply. She added, "Have you two spoken since…?"

"No," I answered quickly. "And I intend to keep it that way. He knows I'm dark. I know he knows, and he knows I have the sword. Not much else to say."

"Grey…"

"What?" I asked. "I told him if I go 'full dark mage, take-over-the-world-mental,' he'd better make sure to put me down."

"That's not the answer."

"It is for me," I said. "I'd do the same for him—and he knows it."

"I sensed a strange energy signature in the park," Rox said, after a pause. "It was a rummer, but it wasn't. It was immense. Then…it was gone."

"Could be the entity that controlled the rummers," I answered, keeping my voice even. "I never got to see Fluffy, but it was there in the dark."

"Fluffy? What's a fluffy?"

"It's what I called whatever was out there," I said. "It was a little shy about sharing its name."

"And you named it Fluffy?"

"Seemed appropriate at the time."

I still avoided mentioning the rummogre. If I shared that information, she'd shift into full-blown 'Sorceress Mom' mode, and order me off the streets for the night. Normally I would ignore her, but she had the power to back up the threats she made. I couldn't imagine a scenario where fighting her turned out well for either of us.

"I gave Street a sedative, and I placed him in stasis," she said. "He should be back to normal in the morning."

"Street doesn't do normal," I said, with a tight smile. "Where's Koda?"

"She's downstairs in the cafeteria," Rox said. "Do you feed that child? I swear she ate her own weight in food."

I nodded. "She has a fast metabolism. Tell her—" Another call interrupted my conversation with a specific tone—The Dive. "One sec, Rox. Cole is calling."

I put it through.

"Speak," I said.

"Grey, you need to get down here...now," Cole said. "You have a *guest*."

"What kind of guest?"

"The kind that wears black suits, looks average, and belongs to some unknown government agency."

"Shit, I'm on my way."

I reconnected to Rox.

"How bad is it?" Rox asked. "Cole never calls unless it's urgent."

"Government agent in The Dive," I said. "I don't recall bumping into any agents recently."

"Did he say which agency?"

"Are there any good ones when it comes to me?"

"Point taken," Rox said. "Don't piss them off, Grey. Do you hear me?"

"Loud and clear," I said. "Do I look like I would start trouble with the government?"

"Do I really need to answer that?"

"Tell Koda I'll meet her at The Dive after she finishes stuffing her face."

I stepped on the accelerator, and let the Beast tear down the street.

NINE

I arrived at The Dive twenty minutes later.

On the way downtown, I'd managed to catalog at least three agencies that would want to have 'a word' with me due to my recent activities. I heard the engine of the Shroud approach as I locked the Beast. I looked down the street, but didn't see Koda.

She had managed to somehow activate the camouflage while riding the bike, something I had never managed to pull off. Her abilities were off-the-charts scary most of the time, and full-blown frightening every other moment.

One day, I'd have her look at the runes on the Beast and see if she could undo them. If she did, we could find a way to destroy it. Not that I was in any hurry, but I recognized the danger presented by the Beast. Even I had a healthy respect for it, and for some reason it liked me enough not to try to kill me.

Koda materialized a few seconds later. The fact that she was a runic cipher, and could ride the Shroud camouflaged, meant she could effectively disappear, and neutralize any tracking tech or spell. She could be next to a target without giving away her location. Like I said, off-the-charts scary.

"A bus is going to squash you if you keep doing that," I said as she locked the Shroud. "They can't see or sense you."

"Just the way I like it," she said, adjusting her rune-covered leathers and removing her kinetics. "I'm practicing stealth running *Dead Sexy*."

"Dead Sexy? Is that the state you're going for, weaving in and out of traffic? Squashed but good-looking?"

"*Dead Sexy* is the new name of the bike *and* my boots. Both make me look…?

"Dead Sexy?"

"Exactly," she said with a nod.

"Until a car cuts you off, then it's just dead," I said, shaking my head. "At the very least, let them see your lights."

"Defeats the purpose of *stealth* running," she said. "What went down at the park? You had Roxanne using some of her choicer curses. I swear, she seemed about five minutes away from heading to the park herself."

"Later," I said, pressing the runes on the door to deactivate the defenses. "We have a serious issue to deal with."

"Connected to Redrum?"

"I really hope not," I answered, stepping into The Dive. "If it is, we are in deeper shit than I imagined."

She stepped in behind me and closed the door.

The Dive attracted a specific kind of clientele, and had recently become a de facto neutral zone for the supernatural community. As large as the Dark Council was, there were plenty of supernaturals and magic-users who preferred not to be associated with them.

The building was located in what was once called Alphabet City, on 4th Street between Avenue C and

D. The neighborhood had changed recently into a cross between upscale and pretentious, with transplants coming in from other parts of the city and buying property to add a new flavor to Lower Manhattan.

It wasn't working out well. Either that, or I was becoming the old man of the neighborhood, and would soon find myself screaming at people to pick up their trash and stay off his property.

I owned The Dive and used it as my informal base of operations.

Mostly, it served as a supernatural bar. Think Cheers, but where nobody wanted to know your name, nor really cared. Most of the patrons went out of their way to avoid giving that kind of information. I didn't ask, they didn't share. Everyone was happy.

The Dive always tasted like bitter honey to me, the ambient magic a mix of minor traps and lethal failsafes. Today, the light scent of cinnamon joined the mix. I had a small apartment upstairs, and enough runes to fry any magic-user thinking of casting inside its walls.

It also had a state-of-the-art security system to make sure we had all the bases covered. If you wanted to unleash mayhem inside its walls, you'd find ample amounts of pain waiting to convince you otherwise.

There was only one rule in The Dive: Drink in peace, or leave in pieces. Frank, the resident mage lizard, made sure the rule was enforced. The Dive's security was three layers deep. Runes for supernaturals, tech for normals, and when everything else went to hell, Frank. Of the three, Frank was the most dangerous, and the most volatile.

TEN

"You have a guest," Cole said from behind the bar. He indicated to the corner with a look. "Says he needs to speak to you."

Frank flicked his tail on the counter, causing electric sparks to fly everywhere. I leaned up against the bar and grabbed one of the rune-covered rags, tossing it on the small flames that resulted from Frank's agitations.

"What did you do now, and how pissed-off are they?" Frank asked, glaring at me. "This guy is screaming government suit."

"I didn't do anything, at least nothing I'll admit to," I said. "I don't know who he is, or who he represents."

"I need a shower," Koda said, heading to the stairs. "Haven always makes me feel like I caught something, every time I visit."

"It's too bad you can't wash off that severe case of PITA," Frank said, scurrying to the other end of the bar as Koda glared. "If only there were a cure for obnoxious, arrogant, unemployed cleaners…. A shame."

"Did anyone hear that squeaking?" Koda asked, putting a hand to her ear while looking around. "It sounded like a mage with phenomenal cosmic power residing in an itty-bitty lizard."

"Dragon! Dragon! Not lizard. I don't do that tongue thing," Frank yelled, flicking his tongue. "Get it straight, Lockpick."

Koda returned a one-finger salute as she climbed the stairs.

"It's good to see you two bonding," I said, rubbing my temple against the low-level pain. "Now I know why my head hurts all the time."

"That's easy," Frank snapped. "Little brain, excess room. It keeps bouncing around in there, giving you mini-concussions."

"And here I thought it was my condition. Maybe we should rename this place, *The Migraine?*"

"You brought that on yourself. I told you to leave the Lockpick to Hades."

"Oh, you think she's the *only* cause of my aggravation?"

"Of course," Frank answered. "I know it's not me. I'm the definition of decorum."

Frank spat on the bar, causing another small bonfire. I threw a rag on it, dousing the flames as the rag glowed orange.

"That...is a nasty habit, lizard."

"What did you call me?"

"You heard me."

"He said it was urgent," Cole said, interrupting the start of our skirmish without looking at us. He was underneath the bar, fixing some of the bottles and putting some of our recent inventory away. He glanced up and stood with a grunt. "By the way, you look like hell."

"Thanks," I said. "It's always urgent. I need a Deathwish, ASAP."

"Normal or extreme?"

"Extreme, heavy on the death."

"That bad out there?" Frank asked, settling down.

I nodded. "Worse," I said. "I just tangoed with some kind of hybrid thing. Half-rummer, half-ogre. All menace."

"An ogrummer...no, that isn't it. An ogrerum?" Frank asked as arcs of power danced across his body, his tail flicking side to side rapidly. We were all on edge tonight. "Where was this?"

"Park. Bethesda Terrace," I said. "Right after I met Street, and some poor mage who didn't make it."

"The ogrerum got him?"

"Rummogre. No," I answered, my voice hard. "There's something else out there in the night. Something that can control rummers, and make dangerous and deadly hybrid creatures."

"Well, shit," Frank answered. "Isn't it time for our yearly vacation?"

"We don't take yearly vacations," I said. "We don't take vacations...period."

"Then we are *way* overdue."

"Nice try, not happening," I said, looking at the man sitting in a dark corner. "Cole, did you vet our guest?"

"He's a ghost," Cole replied. "Not like Koda, but no real footprint...anywhere."

"You sure it's government?"

"Smells like Division 13."

"Shit, really?" I asked. "I thought they didn't exist."

"He looks pretty real," Frank said. "Want me to blast him just to make sure?"

"Let's hold off on the welcome blasting for now," I said. "If he's D13, that will make things worse."

"I'm pretty sure it's Division 13." Cole tapped the side of his nose. "The scent is familiar, and my nose rarely fails."

The fact that Cole even knew about Division 13 spoke volumes. I knew he wasn't just a bartender-restaurant manager. We didn't get into past lives much at The Dive. It was a modern, *Rick's Cafe Americain*, and yes, I was its Rick. If you made it through the doors, you needed to be here. No questions asked. Everyone left me alone, and I returned the favor.

Division 13 was the magical community's equivalent of MI6 or CIA. They dealt with global magical situations, or 'events' as they liked to call them. Being based everywhere, they stepped in when needed and worked from the shadows. Very few supernaturals knew of their existence, until they crossed a line—like casting an entropic dissolution spell in the city and killing their partner.

When they did introduce themselves, it was usually because the supernatural in question needed a corrective measure. On occasion it was a fatal corrective, but no one could ever prove it.

Night Wardens had dealt with them in the past, being a fringe group of magic-users on a scale of power above most, except maybe the Dark Council. No direct oversight meant we attracted attention— early and often.

If Division 13 was paying me a visit, someone was beating the bushes. It also meant they could have information about who or what was killing mages in my city. I'd have to be tactful, but not before my Deathwish. I didn't *people* well before coffee, unless that meant blasting them with Fatebringer.

I glanced at the corner where my guest sat. I made

him wait until Cole slid my coffee down the bar. Considering how I felt after the rummogre, waiting for my Deathwish was my small act of mercy tonight. I took a few sips of pure caffeine bliss, inhaled the aroma, and let my brain bask in javambrosia goodness. The coffee was a perfect counterpoint to the mix of honey and lemon The Dive always produced.

The possible D13 operative was nondescript and ordinary, just this side of invisible, which was, I guessed, intentional. I sensed an energy signature, but the dampeners in The Dive made it hard to pinpoint what kind of magic-user he was.

From my sources, Division 13 had every kind of magic-user working for them. They were the heavy hitters no one knew about. For all I knew, I could be looking at an Arch Mage. I walked over to his table, cup in hand. He looked up and gave me a nod, motioning to the chair opposite his. The smell of cinnamon wafted gently through the air.

"Sorry to keep you waiting. How can I help you?" I said, outstretching a hand.

"Actually, maybe I can help you," he answered with a firm shake.

I felt a small electrical jolt. "That's some grip."

"Sorry about that," he said. "I'm tech heavy. Sometimes it interacts with the ambient energy signatures."

I looked at my hand, and shook off the tingling sensation. It returned to normal a few seconds later.

"Grey," I said.

"I know," he said as he subtly tapped his forearm, which I guess held one of his 'tech heavy' devices. "One of the last Night Wardens, if not *the* last, and owner-operator of this establishment. Currently, a dark mage in possession of an artifact known as *Kuro kokoro kokutan no ken,* which is loosely translated into 'dark spirit'. A blade of questionable alignment."

"Trust me, there's no question as to its alignment."

"You also took on an apprentice recently, one Koda Fan, even though our records show you mostly work alone."

"Where are these records?" I asked. "I'm curious."

"You also go by the alias of Dragonfly, although it seems that name is not currently in use."

"The ones who used it are hard to reach these days," I said, taking a sip of Deathwish, "but I'm guessing *you* know that."

"I do," he said. "Known associates: Cole, no known last name, who surprisingly has very little information available and made it difficult for us to do a full work-up on him, and one Francis Drake, which I'm guessing is an alias, who, according to what we know, is an enormously powerful mage trapped in a…lizard's body?"

"Don't call him a lizard—seriously."

"Duly noted," he said with a nod. "Items of note: Frank the—?"

"Dragon," I finished, keeping my expression serious. "Not kidding."

"Right, Frank the *dragon* still possesses formidable power, and your apprentice is, as I understand it, a cipher?"

I kept my face impassive. The novelty had worn off when he mentioned my alias.

"Cipher?" I asked. "Is that a new term for 'royal pain in the ass'? If it is, then yes, she is a massive cipher."

"Funny," he said with a smile. "I'll take that as a yes."

"And you are?" I asked. "Sorry, I don't have a

wikigadget attached to my arm, but I'm going to guess…technomancer? You work for one of the agencies that doesn't exist, here to make my life even more exciting than I can bear. Close?"

He raised an eyebrow and nodded with approval. "They said you were sharp."

"As a butterknife."

"Ronin—Mark Ronin," he said. "I need your help stopping the Magekiller."

"The Magekiller?" I asked. "Singular?"

"As far as I can tell, yes," Ronin said. "It seems to be a single entity, but that doesn't mean it operates alone."

"Recruits rummers, ogres, and some hybrid thing that's a mix of the two?"

"Yes," Ronin answered, his voice hard. "There have been other creatures, but they all lead back to the Magekiller and his targets."

"Mages?" I asked. "What about the rummers and the strange hybrids?"

"The rummer-ogre hybrids aren't being created by this entity. It's using existing stock—"

"Stock?" I asked, my rageometer kicking up a notch. "Rummers are people who were given a toxic drug. Some of them were Wardens, and all of them deserve respect."

He raised a hand in surrender. "Sorry," he said. "I didn't mean to sound callous. It's just the default training. Don't get close—"

"Don't get attached," I finished. "I know. Just remember that many of those 'creatures' didn't ask for that outcome."

"I will," he said, and I gave him a hard look. "I do."

"Why are you here, Ronin?" I asked, suddenly tired of this verbal game. "So far, all you've told me is

49

what I already know. I've had what you would call a rough night."

"I know," he said. "I saw what you did at Bethesda Terrace."

"And you didn't think a helping hand would've been appreciated?"

"I was gathering data."

"While I was gathering bruises, thanks," I said, holding up my cup before taking another sip. He was getting on my nerves, and I needed to wrap this up before I said or did something potentially lethal. Then it clicked. "Wait a second."

"Yes," he said, keeping his face an unreadable mask. "I had to make sure."

"You're here because you thought…you thought, *I* may be the Magekiller?"

"Some of my 'superiors' did float that idea, yes."

"Really? Because I was a Night Warden?"

"Dark mage with a darker sword," he started. "On speaking terms with the Hound of Hades, and Hades himself? Your apprentice is basically an unknown entity who has no signature, and this place"—he glanced around—"caters to some…let's just say, questionable clientele. You have to admit, most of it points at you."

"Except for that part where Fluffy tried to kill me with the rummogre tonight," I said, my low voice slicing across the table. "Or did you miss that in your data gathering?"

"I'm going to assume you're calling the Magekiller 'Fluffy'?"

"Magekiller sounds better than Fluffy, but it really hates Fluffy," I said with an evil smile. "Did you miss the attempted mage squashing by the rummogre?"

"I didn't, which is why it's just me sitting here having this conversation with you, and not several squads of highly trained agents storming your place of business and home."

"Why me, again?"

"Without exception, every victim has been a mage," he answered. "The only one...the only mage, who has survived an encounter with it—is you."

ELEVEN

"**D**o you know what it is?"

"Our best guess is that you faced an ancient being that goes by the name of Mr. Dark."

"Mr. Dark?" I asked, incredulous. "Are you shitting me?"

"No, I'm not."

"Why not just call it the *Bogeyman,* or *El Cuco?*"

Ronin remained silent for a few seconds, and then sighed. "This thing is old...older than we can imagine."

"Fine, you've given me names, but *what* is it?" I asked. "How can it mask an entire area until I was surrounded by rummers? How did it control the rummers and the rummogre?"

"I...we...don't know for sure," he answered. "I can tell you similarities we've found."

"Enlighten me."

"Are you familiar with the works of Professor Ziller?"

"Do you know a mage who isn't?"

"Good point. Anyway, a few years ago, he wrote a paper on the properties of 'darkness' and how, in certain cases, and within a specific context, 'darkness' develops sentience. Ziller called it, *On Darkness and Fear—The Sentience of Dark Entities, and the Correlation to Fear Responses*."

"I've never read or heard of this paper."

"I know," Ronin said. "Certain Elders of certain sects freaked out when they read his paper, and they suppressed it."

"But you managed to get a copy?"

"Yes," he said. "I did get a copy, from Ziller himself, and I can see why they were disturbed."

"Let me guess," I said. "Fear and the use of dark magic somehow creates these entities or helps them exist?"

"Not quite, but not very far off either."

"And you think…?"

"Have you ever heard of pavormancy?"

"It's one of the fringe disciplines," I said, "based on fear or manipulating fear responses?"

"A pavormancer can induce or control targets through their fears," Ronin said with a nod. "Rare, but quite powerful as far as disciplines go."

"You think this thing is some kind of pavormancer?"

"Did you see the victim?" Ronin asked, his voice grim. "The one in the park? Did he look like he died a peaceful death?"

"Not in the least," I said, looking into the darkness of my cup. "Whatever finished him, scared him to death."

"In this case, literally."

"It tried to play the fear angle with me too," I recalled. "Sounded surprised when I didn't spook."

Ronin nodded. "Every victim I've encountered looks like they were scared shitless," he said. "Whatever this thing does, it uses fear to attack."

"It must use latent fear," I said. "And since my life

is such a paradise of rainbows and unicorns, I don't have much to fear."

"That's probably the only reason you somehow managed to survive your encounter with the Magekiller," Ronin said. "You don't exhibit fear, and you're a dark mage. I doubt it's a coincidence."

"It's thin," I said, feeling the pounding in my head subside, as the caffeine wrangled the stampeding horses in my skull. "That rummogre was definitely trying to pound the life out of me."

"Thin, probably," Ronin answered. "Fact is, you're the only one who crossed its path and remained unbroken."

The image of the mage's broken body flashed in my mind.

"What kind of magic-user are you?" I asked.

"Excuse me?"

"I can sense your energy, but my defenses in here are scattering your signature."

"That's not your defenses." He touched the device on his arm that looked like a cross between a phone and futuristic tech. After a few seconds, his signature came across clearly.

"I was right. You're a technomancer," I said with a satisfied nod. "My guy at the bar, Cole, says you're Division 13. Is he right?"

Ronin narrowed his eyes, glancing over at the bar.

"What do you know about your *guy*, Cole?"

"All I *need* to know," I said, letting the menace slip into my voice. "He keeps this place running, and he has my back...always. More importantly, he's my friend."

"I can neither confirm nor deny my involvement with Division 13," Ronin said after a few moments. "If such an agency did exist, and I'm not saying it does, they would be concerned that your guy, Cole, knows about it."

"Sounds like a yes," I said.

Ronin shrugged in response. "Take it any way you'd like. You may want to have a word with Cole about how he possesses that information, though. I'd hate to see your place of business and home destroyed."

"Is that a threat?"

"Division 13 doesn't do subtle," Ronin answered. "If they felt he was a security risk, they would erase this place, with all of you in it, and call it a magic gone wrong."

"Destroying The Dive would be an accident?"

"You know those dark mages," Ronin said, "always casting those dangerous spells, like entropic dissolutions."

"Fuck you."

"Don't get it twisted, Grey," he said. "Division 13 thrives because no one really believes it exists. Keeping that narrative intact is a priority."

"We would just be collateral damage?"

"Don't be naive," he said. "They'll make it look like *you* did it."

"Of course, dark mage gone mad," I said. "It almost writes itself."

"You wanted to know the response," Ronin answered. "This will be just another spell that went wrong. A shame, really. Make it a point to speak to Cole."

"I'll do that, and have my defenses calibrated," I said, taking a calming breath. "I can usually tell what the magic-users are in The Dive, even when they're using cutting-edge tech to hide their signatures."

He nodded. "Your defenses are above par. I just

56

like to keep my signature hidden for security reasons and operational readiness."

"Right," I said. "In other words, easier to ambush targets."

"That too," he replied. "Better to be unseen and unremarkable."

"Why are you here, really?" I asked. "D13 has the resources and the manpower to handle this Magekiller without my help."

"Division 13 considers the victims of this entity… how should I put this…non-essential."

"You mean expendable?" I felt the anger rise. "You'll want to pick your next words carefully."

"You have to understand; Division 13 is so large, this case isn't even on their radar," Ronin said, the frustration coming through in his voice. "They get so caught up looking at the beam—"

"They miss the splinter," I said. "Sounds like the Wardens once upon a time. So, go to the Dark Council."

"Not viable. They're dealing with a leadership restructuring. Not to mention their factions are barely holding it together. Whoever thought vampires, weres, and mages made a smooth, functioning body, must have been insane."

"Probably looked good on paper," I answered. "But you're right, they don't play well together."

"Without Nakatomi's presence, it's going to get worse," Ronin said. "Her brother doesn't wield the same influence, and you currently possess the only other deterrent."

"Don't even think about it," I said, shaking my head. "The Dark Council and I don't mix—ever."

"Understood. Division 13 will take care of it."

"What else do you know about this 'Mr. Dark'?" I asked.

"I was hoping you could tell me."

I stared at him for a few seconds.

"I'm guessing you have access to an insane amount of information, to the point that you could probably tell me how many hairs are on my ass."

"That's just…no, I don't know how many hairs are on your ass," he answered with a look of disgust. "What's wrong with you?"

"The jury's still out on that one."

"How is ass hair even relevant?"

"Good point. D13 is a technological powerhouse. Why don't you wiki this?"

"Because this is ancient knowledge. It's not going to be in some database."

"Then your people are slacking," I said. "This info should be available at the touch of a few buttons."

This time it was his turn to stare.

"It doesn't always work like that, and you know this," he said, shaking his head. "I don't have the access a dark mage has."

I knew where he was going. "Aria won't let you near her library, not while you're breathing, at least. She barely tolerates me."

"Wasn't talking about the Wordweavers."

I didn't know where he was going before, but I did now. "No. Are you suicidal?" I asked. "He's just as strong, if not stronger, than Aria, and a lot crankier."

"That's why I'm asking *you*."

"Why don't you ask him?" I shot back.

"I'm not a dark mage, you are," he replied. "There are parts of the Archive he keeps off-limits. Even to me."

"For a very good reason," I said. "Most of those tomes and grimoires are lethal."

"I think the information I'm looking for is in there, but I need a dark mage."

"We aren't exactly on speaking terms," I said, shaking my head. "You don't know what you're asking."

"Actually, I do," Ronin answered with a sigh. "He's my best and only chance."

I shook my head again, and took a long drink of coffee. Honor and I had had a *conversation* a few years ago. It didn't end well. I damaged part of the Archive, and we'd agreed to mutually avoid blasting each other to bits.

"You know he's an Archmage, right?" I asked. "Or at least as strong as one."

"I know he's strong."

"I'll ask," I said. "You'd better have a hell of a peace offering."

"I think I do," Ronin said, pulling out a small book. The title read: *On Darkness and Fear—The Sentience of Dark Entities, and the Correlation to Fear Responses.*"

"Shit," I said under my breath. "How did you get a copy of that? I thought they were all destroyed?"

"There's only one other copy, and Professor Ziller has it," Ronin said, "He gave me this copy."

I rested a hand lightly on the book. The latent energy thrummed through my fingers. This book was dangerous. He slid it across the table to me.

"What are you doing?" I said, sliding it back. "You give it to him."

"I'm offering you a chance to help me *and* repair your relationship with Honor," Ronin said. "It makes sense to be able to access the Archive. You know I'm right."

"Bullshit. You're using me to get information on the Magekiller, because Honor won't let you into that part of the Archive."

"Well, that too," he answered. "I think he's forgotten what happened between you two by now."

"Do you know Honor?" I asked. "Books were destroyed."

"He is a bit particular about his books," Ronin answered. "But this should help smooth things over. I'll let him know to expect you."

"Wait, you said *you* were asking," I said, recalling his earlier words. "You aren't here as Division 13?"

"Yes and no."

"That sounds like you've gone rogue."

"Officially, I'm on extended leave."

"And unofficially?"

"I'm sanctioned to do whatever needs to get done, while giving Division 13 plausible deniability," he said with a smile. "Win-win for me."

He stood and tapped his arm-computer.

"Is that thing only for technomancers?"

"More or less," he said. "We have to bond to it on several levels, but they can be removed, unlike a certain artifact that has joined to a certain dark mage."

"I have no idea what you're talking about."

"I'm sure you don't," he said, handing me a card. "If you come across the Magekiller on your patrols, give me a call. I won't just be gathering data this time."

"I appreciate it," I said, taking the plain, blank white card and turning it over. "How am I supposed to read this?"

"Ask the lizard," he said. "I have other leads to follow. Understand, just because Division 13 doesn't interact with the Wardens any longer, doesn't mean—"

"They aren't watching me," I finished. "Tell them to take a number."

"As long as you remain a dark mage, they'll keep an eye on you," Ronin said.

"I'm flattered, really."

"Don't be. They've been burned by dark mages in the past. In some cases, literally."

"So, I'm not being watched by fans?" I asked. "Now, I'm slightly disappointed."

"There are some in the organization who think Wardens are a relic that should be retired, permanently," Ronin answered. "Don't give them a reason to act."

"I may be old, but it doesn't mean I'm helpless."

"That was evident tonight. I'd prefer we focus on the Magekiller, and whoever is flooding the streets with this new Redrum X."

"Tell your people to leave me and mine alone, and we'll avoid the pain," I said. "If they don't start none, won't be none."

"'Don't start none, won't be none'?" Ronin asked. "Really? What is this, kindergarten?"

"Sometimes the simplest messages are best," I said with a slight smile. "Tell them to back off, so I don't have to shoot them. Dead operatives make my life messy. I don't like messy."

"I'll inform them to leave you alone." He made to leave. "They won't listen, you know."

"I know," I said. "But I'll feel better knowing they were warned when I shoot them."

"Maybe you should get out more? Take up a hobby?"

"I get out…every night."

"I meant besides these patrols you do," Ronin said. "I know they're called the Night Wardens, but you are allowed to do things during the day. Take a break, Grey. Next thing you know, you'll be running around claiming to 'be the night,' or some other insanity."

"Right, and I'm the one who needs to get out more?" I asked. "Before you go, I wanted to ask you who's making the new strain of Redrum?"

"Your guess is as good as mine," Ronin answered, his voice hard. "Surprisingly, it's not on any task lists that I know of."

"UV-resistant rummers aren't a priority for Division 13?" I asked in disbelief. "Really? What are they waiting for? Until rummers fill the streets?"

"Wake up, Grey," Ronin said. "Think about the population it's hitting the hardest."

"The homeless and forgotten," I said. "They view this as a culling, population control…bastards."

"Exactly," Ronin answered. "They aren't going to devote resources to finding the supplier, but I'm guessing you will."

"I will."

"When you find whoever it is, do me a favor?"

"What?" I asked. "Hand him over to the authorities? Because I can tell you right now that—"

"Put a few extra rounds in them from me."

I nodded, surprised at his words. "Will do."

"One more thing," he said. "When it looks like you're walking into a trap, and you don't know who to trust—use the number."

"What number?" I said, looking at the card. "Not seeing a number."

"You will."

Ronin walked away from the table and left The Dive. I found myself not disliking him entirely. He was still part of Division 13, which meant hidden agendas were par for the course.

Still, better the devil you know than the devil you don't. I turned over the blank card he had given me, put Ziller's book in my duster pocket, and headed back over to the bar.

TWELVE

I tossed the card on the table, next to Frank.

"Can you read that?" I asked. "Looks blank to me."

"Maybe it's time you finally admitted your age and got some glasses," Frank answered. "You could be the scholarly Night Warden."

"Can you read it or not?"

"Give me a second," Frank answered, examining the card. "The suit gave you this?"

I nodded. "You know what I really need? Besides another cup?"

I slid my mug down the bar. Cole stopped it and removed it from the bar in one deft move.

"What did he want?" Cole asked, as he refilled my mug. "He left in a hurry."

"He wanted to let me know that he knew—about me, and all of you," I said. "I think you spooked him."

Cole raised an eyebrow and slid my mug back. Gary B. B. Coleman came over the sound system to let me know the sky was crying. I paused a moment to enjoy his voice, savoring the fresh java.

"I spooked him?" Cole asked. "Can't see how."

"Apparently he couldn't get much info on you," I

63

said. "The fact that you guessed he was D13, threw him."

Cole nodded with a slight smile, and tapped the side of his nose.

"Told you," he said. "Never fails."

"He said to make sure you kept your information to yourself," I answered. "D13 is twitchy about people knowing they exist."

"Might come over and erase your ass, Cole," Frank said with a chuckle, until he saw my expression. "Shit, really?"

"He wouldn't be the only one," I said, pointing to the card. "Can you read it or not? For the record, you're older than I am."

"There is no way you could possibly know that," Frank snapped. "Yes, I can read it. It just needs a special treatment."

"If you say saliva, I'd prefer you leave it blank, thanks."

"Did he tell you to give it to me?" Frank asked, flicking his tail side to side.

I nodded. "Said: 'Give it to the tiny lizard with delusions of grandeur. He'll know what to do,'" I answered. "Having my doubts now."

"I need to send a charge through it," Frank answered. "But you can't be in proximity when I do it, or it will fry you too."

"Fine. Take it upstairs and do what you need to do."

"Be right back."

A second later, Frank disappeared with a small thunderclap. Upstairs, I heard a crack of lightning followed by another, louder, thunderclap. A few moments later, the smell of chlorine assaulted my senses, and Frank reappeared on the bar.

"Wonderful. It smells like a pool in here, thanks."

Frank tossed me the card. "It only smells that way to you," he said, with a growl. "And, you're welcome."

I picked up the card. It was covered in runes. They looked ancient and unfamiliar.

"I'm supposed to be able to read this?"

"Yes," Frank said. "If you focus, you can."

I looked down at the card again and narrowed my eyes, letting my inner sight read the runes. It was a string of digits I didn't recognize.

"All of that security for a phone number?" I asked, looking at the number again. "Seems kind of long. This international?"

Frank looked down at the card. "My guess is that it connects directly to that super tech on his arm."

I nodded. "It makes sense," I said, sliding my mug down to Cole, who dropped it in the sink. "Still seems long."

I put the card in a pocket and grabbed a rune-covered rag, just in case.

"What did he want?" Frank asked. "I mean, besides giving you his number and threatening us?"

I pulled out Ziller's book.

Frank took a step back. "Whoa," he said. "Where did you get that?"

"I have to go see Honor."

The words hung in the air for a few seconds.

"Well," Frank said, after letting out a long breath, "it was nice knowing you. Cole and I will keep the place going after you're gone. Maybe even rename it —The Grey Dive. What do you think, Cole?"

"Has a nice ring to it," Cole answered. "Maybe a small statue, or just hang the duster in a corner as an homage to our departed friend."

"That's a nice touch. I like the hanging duster, but over there in the other corner, out of the way. Don't want anyone falling into it by accident and getting lost."

"Good point," Cole said, nodding as he wiped down the bar. "What about Koda?"

"We'll keep the Lockpick," Frank said. "Someone still needs to keep the streets safe. I'll go out with her."

"Really?" I deadpanned. "You and Koda will go out and patrol?"

"To honor the spirit of the brainless Night Warden who went to the Archive and got himself blasted. It's the least we can do."

"You won't make it out the door without killing each other," I said, picking up the book. "Besides, Honor won't kill me, at least not before I give him this. Make the call."

"You're serious?" Cole asked. "Should I give Roxanne a heads-up? You know… just in case?"

I glared at Cole. "You think I'm looking forward to this? Call him."

Cole headed to the back room.

"Nothing good will come of this, Grey," Frank said with a flick of his tail. He was about to spit when I threw a runed rag on him. He shook it off. "Funny. I hope Honor does blast your ass. That's what you need and deserve."

"You know what I really need?" I said.

Koda came downstairs silently and scowled at Frank, who deliberately ignored her by turning away.

"What do you need?" Koda asked. "Besides a new form of security that's less…lizardly."

"Shut it, Lockpick."

"I need a warden bag."

Frank groaned, and moved to the other end of the bar.

THIRTEEN

"What's a warden bag?"

"What are you doing?" Frank hissed. "Don't encourage him."

Cole appeared a few seconds later. "The call has been placed," he said. "If he wants to erase—I mean, see—you, he'll call back. Who knows, maybe he's mellowed with age?"

Frank glanced at Cole, and shook his tail. "Did you smack your head on the doorframe on the way back?" Frank asked. "Mages don't get 'mellow' with age, unless that means cranky, angry, and irritable."

"Maybe he won't call?"

Very few people could approach the Central Archive directly. Honor set up a system, where if you wanted access, you would reach out and leave a message. If he was feeling social that day, or you were important enough, you'd get a call back. I didn't expect a call.

"Did I hear you right?" Cole asked, a smile barely crossing his lips. "You were asking about a warden bag, Koda?"

Frank hissed at Cole.

"What?" Koda asked, innocently. "Is this bag cursed?"

Frank glared at her and shook his tail again. "Why are you asking? Now he'll never shut up."

"Looks like we're low on the Deathwish," Cole said, heading down the stairs. "I think I need to check the inventory. Be right back."

"Sure, run while you can, traitor," Frank said. "You know exactly how much inventory we have at all times."

"I may have miscalculated a few boxes," Cole answered with a smile. "Better safe than sorry, especially with Mr. Cranky Mage and Deathwish."

"I won't forget this, Brutus."

"What's a warden bag?" Koda asked. "Is that like an accessory? Can I get one?"

Frank turned to look at her.

"Are you brain-damaged?" Frank asked. "Stop asking questions."

"Didn't you say they couldn't be made anymore, Frank?" Cole yelled from the top of the stairs. "Remember?"

"You bastard," Frank said, whirling in Cole's direction as he disappeared down the stairs. "Et tu, Cole? Really?"

"Why not?" Koda asked, and Frank sighed.

"Fine," Frank answered. "I'll school the young Sith. You"—he pointed a finger in my direction —"shut your face."

"Sith?" Koda asked, confused. "I'm not a Sith. If anything I'm a Je—"

"He's a dark mage," Frank finished, pointing at me. He turned to Koda. "You're his apprentice, ergo that makes you a Sith."

"He kind of has a point," I said, nodding. "You do act very Sithy, what with the anger and hate. Jedis are

68

very peaceful warriors, unlike a certain Night Warden apprentice I know, who gives in to the anger on a regular basis."

"Shit," Koda said, glaring at Frank.

"That's just a scrambled Sith," Frank said, with a flick of his tail. "Just like you. Now, pay attention, because I'm only explaining this once."

"Fine, warden bags," Koda said. "Enlighten me, *dragon*."

Koda knew just how to nudge Frank. Nothing pleased him more than being called a dragon. He shook his tail, as small arcs of energy flew off his body. I tossed the rag on the most volatile, preventing a small fire.

"Back in the day, when Wardens patrolled the night and kept the city safe, the concept of time and relative distance in space was new. Wardens carried everything they needed in specially designed bags."

"Warden bags," Koda answered. "And they were special because…?"

"They were created to hold everything a warden needed on patrol."

"What do you mean 'hold everything'?" Koda asked. "How big were these things? I'm not carrying a duffel bag on patrol."

"About attache-case size, at least on the outside," Frank said. "Inside? I heard a Warden got lost in his own bag. They never did find him."

"They're like your coat pockets?" Koda pointed at my duster. "Bigger on the inside?"

"Better," Frank said. "Warden bags acted as portals, containment, offense, and defense. They were virtually indestructible."

"So why are they so hard to get now?"

"Well," Frank said, "they had a small flaw."

"A small flaw?" Koda asked. "How small?"

"If they suffered catastrophic damage, they would implode."

"That doesn't sound so—"

"Swallowing everything and everyone in proximity," Frank added, his voice grim. "Starting with the Warden wearing the bag."

"What the fuck?" Koda said, looking at me. "And you want this bag, why?"

"Frank missed a few features," I said, looking at the lizard hard. "Didn't you, *dragon*?"

"Nope, can't say that I did," he said, flicking his tail nervously. "Portals, containment, offense, and defense. Covered it all."

"I'll take it from here, Professor Omission," I said. "Warden bags were keyed to each warden. No two bags were the same, and you could only use your own bag. They also had the capacity to act as translators, null zones with camouflage, and signature masking."

"Like a cipher?" Koda asked, raising an eyebrow.

"Exactly like a cipher, just not built in like you have it," I said. "They also—if the Night Warden was a powerful enough mage—allowed the Warden to plane-walk without casting."

"That does sound sweet," Koda said. "As long as it doesn't implode on you, you're golden with a bag like that."

"One more thing," I said, looking at Frank, who glared back. "Each bag was a repository for the spells you knew. More than that, it could store knowledge and make it accessible to the owner."

"How much knowledge?" Koda asked. "How many gigabytes?"

"Gigabytes?" I asked. "This isn't a computer. It's a—"

"It was the equivalent of one zettabyte of

information," Frank answered. "That's what made it dangerous. All that information contained in one place with few fail-safes, except the warden who owned it? What do you think happened? Want to share that part, bag-boy?"

"What happened?" Koda asked.

"Tell her how the bags helped destroy the Wardens and cost you…everything."

"Grey," Koda started. "You don't have to…I mean if it's that bad."

"No," I said, keeping my voice steady and shoving the memories away. "He's right, you should get the entire history."

"It's okay, really."

"Some of the stronger, more powerful Wardens wanted more information," I said, my voice hard. "Spells they didn't have access to. A group of them formed, and started stealing bags."

"I thought you said each bag was keyed to its owner?"

"I did."

"Oh…shit."

I nodded. "In order to get the information, they tortured the weaker wardens to force them to divulge the knowledge of each bag."

"Did it work?"

"It was too much information," I said. "The tortured wardens could barely remember their own names, much less the information in the bag."

"What did they do?"

"They crossed a line that shouldn't have been crossed," I replied. "They used a siphon spell, one of the darkest spells known to mages, to basically 'download' the information directly into their own bags."

"That worked?" Koda said. "Damn, what the hell was wrong with them?"

"It did," Frank said, looking at me. "Except for one thing. The siphon worked too well. It left the subject-warden braindead. It was too much for them, and their minds broke. Another group of wardens got together to stand against the greedy fuckers. They ended up casting an entropic dissolution."

"That was—?"

"Yes," I said with a nod. "We stopped them, even though we couldn't save or revert the tortured wardens. Then we lost control of the spell."

"This is why you don't need a warden bag," Frank said quietly. "You have your coat. What else do you need besides deep pockets?"

"There was one more feature, but it was only a rumor," I said. "Some of the most powerful bags, the ones with the accumulated knowledge of several wardens, began to evolve, connecting rudimentary spells into deeper unknown spells—powerful spells."

"What the hell do you need an evolving bag for?"

"To deal with evolving rummers, and other creatures living in the darkness," I said with steel lacing my words. "The Dark Council, NYTF…none of the other groups are capable or willing to meet the threat on the street. Even D13 is staying out of it."

"Have you tried the other Council?" Frank asked. "You may as well if you're going to see Honor."

"You know I can't do that," I said. "They have a KOS order on me."

"You really do know how to make friends," Frank said. "I may know someone who can get you a bag, or at least make the introduction."

"Who?"

"Are you sure you need this bag? Notice I didn't say want."

"Yes," I said, after a moment of thought. "A warden bag would make the patrols easier. They carry everything I need and more."

"You sure I can't convince you to wear a utility belt?"

"Warden bag, lizard. Not utility belt."

"No need to get personal," Frank said. "I'm just asking, and it's a 'no' on the other Council?"

"I'd rather not test if the 'Kill on Sight' order is still active, if that's okay with you."

"Just asking."

I glared at him. "It's going to be a 'yes' on shooting you, if you keep this up."

"Once I start this process, there's no halfway, understood?"

"Understood," I said. "This had better not be sending me to Tessa."

"You're going to wish it was at the Moving Market."

"Where and who?"

"You need to go to Fordey Boutique," Frank said. "Speak to LD and TK if you really want a warden bag. If anyone has one, it would be them."

"Fuck me," I said, as Cole appeared behind the bar. "Are you serious? Fordey?"

"The only place," Frank said. "Still need a bag?"

"If they have one, yes," I said. "Find out if they really have one, and I'll make the trip."

I sensed the power shift and moved to the other end of the bar.

<You prefer a bag over me?>

I knew Izanami would say something…it was only a matter of time.

"Is that a real question?"

I noticed Koda glance at Frank. "Sword?" she asked.

Frank nodded, waving a finger in a circle near his head. "Psychosword."

<Of course, or else I would not ask it.>

She was pretty damn literal for a goddess in a sword.

"Yes, I do," I said. "It's a warden bag, and I'm a Warden."

<This bag will not keep you alive. I am a weapon and a goddess.>

"Modest much?" I asked. "It can, and it's an inanimate object. I don't have to worry about it one day going on a rampage trying to devour backpacks or clutches."

<You must work on your attempts at levity. Even I can do better, and I do not possess this thing you call a 'sense of humor'.>

"Just got the call," Cole said, the surprise evident in his voice. "Honor will see you."

"If he agreed, I'd better get prepared…just in case he's feeling nostalgic and wants to blast me. I'll be down in ten, get ready."

"I was born ready," Koda answered. "I'm waiting for you, old man."

"Respect your elders," I said. "Before I jettison you out of here."

I headed up the stairs, and overheard Koda.

"There's another Council?" Koda asked, confused. "Since when?"

"Since he became a dark mage," Frank said. "And nearly killed everyone."

"What did they form, a darker Council?"

"They created something to deal with the darkness, not embrace it," Frank answered. "They created the Light Council."

FOURTEEN

F rank was a master of exaggeration, as usual.

The warden bags didn't destroy the Night Wardens. They facilitated the Night Wardens' undoing, but they didn't destroy them. If there was ever one event that nearly destroyed the Night Wardens, it was the Purge.

The supernatural community had felt the Wardens were too much of an obstacle. They joined to combat their common enemy, and destroyed Shadow Helm, along with more than half of the Night Wardens, in a bloody year of warfare. I'd lost many good friends that year. We'd finally convinced the supernaturals that it was better to live with us than die by our hands, but the damage was done. The decimation of the Night Wardens forced us into the shadows.

Soon after, the formation of the NYTF and the Dark Council made Night Wardens redundant, and they were disbanded, except for a small token force. It was after the Purge that wardens, feeling desperate, started stealing bags.

The Light Council was not created as a response to my turning dark. It was created as a response to what happened with the warden bags. The Light Council was made up of Mages, Shapeshifters, and Archives. Their existence was less known than Division 13, which made them—for all intents and purposes—non-existent.

That is, until you destroyed several of the treasured books in their library. Then they were very real, as was the pain they could inflict.

Honor, who led the Light Council, happened to be a mage and an Archive. Similar to the Living Libraries, Archives could access an immense amount of knowledge.

Unlike the Living Libraries, the Archives didn't hold the knowledge in their minds. They managed to access the information with the assistance of a Curator, a mage who created a conduit to the knowledge.

All of this had to occur in an actual archive building, which was full of fail-safes and deterrents against attack. This meant the archives could access knowledge on many subjects, without being in danger of being attacked or kidnapped. It was the answer to dealing with the danger the warden bags posed. It was a cumbersome and difficult process, but it worked.

By making the access to information difficult, only the most determined magic-users went in search of it. Aside from your basic spells, and those taught to you by your sect, if you really wanted knowledge, you had to prove it.

Now, most of the wardens were gone. I wasn't naive enough to think I was the last warden. I was, however, the most noticeable. I wasn't hiding. They knew where to find me. Thing was, I was the guard dog everyone hated, but they tolerated me because my presence allowed them to sleep easy at night.

I knew some were still out there in hiding, or doing the same thing I was doing, acting alone and keeping the streets safe, but when it all eventually went to hell, they were going to be knocking on my door.

Lyrra had managed to reduce warden numbers considerably, but I knew she didn't get all of us. I wasn't in a hurry to locate any of them. It wasn't like I'd left the Night Wardens on good terms. By the end, they were comfortable with the idea of ghosting me.

The Light Council was different.

I actively avoided them, which would have been easier if I knew who they were. Outside of Honor and his place—Dragonflies in the Reeds, the Light Council could be anywhere or anyone. Division 13 was amateur hour compared to them. The fact that they had shapeshifters only made it harder.

After they'd issued the kill order, I realized that actively looking for them wasn't in my best interests. I kept away from them as best as I could, and I was sure they kept an eye on me. As long as they didn't try to actively erase me, we were good.

Damn, Frank was right, I really needed to work on my social skills.

I reached the top level of The Dive, and deactivated the runes around my door. Trying to get into my room without shutting down the runes was a futile exercise, unless you were Koda, who could bypass any security measure. Between her and Frank, it was no wonder my headache never left.

I opened my door, and another set of runes thrummed as I entered my room. It was twice the size of the entire third floor. I'd cheated by using the same runes that made the pockets of my coat larger than they actually were. I opened some of the drawers and removed items I might need.

I placed the most important object, Ziller's book, in the center of the pile. For a second, a utility belt didn't sound like such a bad idea. If the book worked, I wouldn't need half of the items. If it didn't, I doubted how long I could hold off Honor. I placed the items in my duster and headed downstairs.

This was turning into a long night, but I preferred not to keep Honor waiting. I was just as surprised as Cole that he'd agreed to a meet. Besides, if I needed to take a trip to Fordey, I wasn't going to do that at night. If I tripped their security, not even my duster would survive that encounter.

FIFTEEN

I descended the stairs and saw them lined up against the bar.

Mighty Sam was lamenting over the sound system about the hurt being over. That's when I noticed the lilies. Cole, Koda, and even Frank held lilies in their hands.

"Give our regards to Honor," Frank said, his voice somber. "You had a good run, Grey."

"Cut the shit," I barked. "You"—I pointed at Koda —"get on your bike and follow me. Frank, get me the info on Fordey and the Warden bag. Cole, check on Street, then contact Aria. Tell her I need to see her. We have a monster out there that can make worse creatures and is preying on mages…homeless mages. Get moving, people."

They all jumped into action. I tightened Fatebringer's holster as I stepped outside and headed to the Beast, my senses expanding, and feeling for Darkspirit. Its darkness was a familiar sensation, as I got into the Beast and started the engine. The loud rumble was answered by the Shroud's engine behind me.

I looked in my rear-view mirror and saw Koda

put on her kinetics and camouflage, fading from sight.

"Make sure you don't get hit by a truck or something," I said, placing my hand on the dash and watching the runes pulse. "Is this still stealth running practice?"

"Exactly," Koda said over the comms. "If you can locate me, dinner is my treat. Now, where are we going?"

"Downtown," I said. "If you follow me—"

"Never mind," she answered quickly. "Found it. Dragonflies in the Reeds takes up half a block on Broadway from Warren to Murray. Right across from City Hall. Meet you there, old man."

"How did you…?"

"Kinetics have an onboard computer with a GPS," she said. "I just tweaked it a bit."

"Wait for me *outside*," I warned. "Honor is expecting me. He won't appreciate you trying to walk in uninvited."

"I'll knock first," she answered with a laugh. "If his security is anything like yours, I can get in with my eyes closed."

Some lessons were best experienced, not explained.

"If you think you can bypass his security," I said, shaking my head, "order me a coffee when you get there. Rahbi makes a mean Deathwish."

Dragonflies in the Reeds was located in downtown Manhattan. In addition to being a neutral location, Dragonflies—as it was known to the general population—was also the Central Archive for the supernatural community. It contained most of the rare and ancient books Aria didn't have in the Cloisters, and some she did.

To call it a library was inaccurate. The Central

Archive was a repository of knowledge. It was also the only place outside of The Dive that served Deathwish coffee. That made my schism with Honor all the more painful, but I enjoyed breathing more than I enjoyed Deathwish, but not by much. Breathing just edged out Deathwish.

I drove downtown, keeping the Beast reined in since traffic was light. The Central Archive, unlike The Dive, was an official neutral zone. As a neutral location, violence of any kind was strictly prohibited within the confines of its walls.

After our conversation, Honor had implemented a one-time infraction rule. Any rule broken once could result in lethal enforcement. The thought brought a small smile to my face. Honor must have been pissed when he thought up that one. I pulled up to the front and parked the Beast, her rumble becoming a purr as I stepped out and locked the doors.

I looked around but didn't see the Shroud, or Koda. Her being a cipher gave her an advantage, but Honor was no ordinary mage. If anyone could sense her, it would be him. I stepped to the door and let it scan me.

I noticed the intricate runic symbols on the doorframe. They were designed to prevent anyone from entering or exiting the Archive, if needed. The entrance I used led to the Central Archive coffee shop. If Koda made it in, I'd get my coffee right away. If she'd gotten caught, I'd still get my coffee, but then I'd get to watch her squirm and wonder how it happened. I was really hoping she'd been caught.

The sweet smell of coffee grounds filled my lungs as the door clicked open.

The interior of the Central Archive reminded me of a large dojo or meditation hall, with heavy Asian influences focused on empty space and wood. Several tiered levels contained rows and rows of books. The center of the floor space contained neatly arranged desks and large tables for study. On every table sat several bankers' lamps with green glass shades.

Most of them were off, and the desks empty. I wondered if Honor expected a repeat of my last visit and had sent everyone home. I stepped into the empty coffee area, which was situated to the rear of the main floor. Behind the counter stood Rahbi, Honor's right-hand woman.

If Honor was the hurricane, Rahbi was the eye in its center. She looked up, gave me a nod and a small smile.

"On the house," she said, placing a large mug on the counter, and pointed with her own mug behind me. "Friend of yours?"

I stepped over to the counter and grabbed my mug of Deathwish. It wouldn't be as potent as the javambrosia Cole created, but it would be close. I glanced at Rahbi and returned the smile. After inhaling the coffee goodness, I turned to see Koda sitting very still behind one of the desks, staring daggers in my direction. I raised my cup in her direction. The smell of cinnamon lingered around me, but I didn't taste any in my coffee.

"Thank you. It's been a while," I said, turning back to Rahbi and taking a sip. "Good to see you."

"And you," she said. Her pale gray eyes bored into mine as she pulled her jet-black hair into a ponytail. "The Archive is closed for the evening, and KOS has been paused for your visit."

"That was generous," I said. "Is he mellowing with age?"

"Once you leave, it goes back into effect. No one

will attack you while on Archive property, but I wouldn't linger outside—accidents happen."

"I'm going to guess that's a 'no' on mellowing?"

"He's in the office," she said, glancing up, "waiting for you. Excuse me while I attend to some matters. Oh, and Grey?"

"Yes?" I said, knowing what was coming…the warning. "I'm not here to settle anything."

"Don't piss him off, and don't break or burn *anything*."

"On my best behavior," I said. "Promise."

"Don't forget who you're speaking to," she said. "Your best behavior sucks."

I really needed to work on my social skills.

She stepped out from behind the counter, and walked across the floor to a staircase leading down. She moved with a lithe grace that disguised a coiled lethality. It was like watching a tigress stalking prey —beautiful and terrifying all at once.

The rumors about her being almost as powerful as Honor were well founded. An angry Rahbi was a lethal and formidable Rahbi. I shuddered at the memory.

She had arrived at the Central Archive the same way Cole came to The Dive, escaping a past they no longer wished to live. I didn't know what it was, and it wasn't my place to ask.

Some things were best left unasked.

SIXTEEN

I could sense him waiting for me.

It only spoke to the power he possessed. Even with the defenses and runes in the Central Archive, I doubted Honor could hide even if he wanted to. He just bled off too much power.

I pulled out Ziller's book, and headed up the staircase next to the coffee shop. I left Koda at the desk, where she sat fuming. She was ensnared by a lattice that would take me days to unravel. Even then, I'd probably get it wrong. That kind of magic was tricky at best. I took what I thought was the safest and wisest course of action for her…and for me: I left her there, and went to see Honor.

The second level of the Archive was reserved for rare books, which were sealed behind magically enhanced glass. If you wanted a rare book, it required either Honor or Rahbi to access the case, before escorting you to a sealed reading room. Several of the books were never allowed out of their cases due to age or risk to the reader.

Honor kept some of the most dangerous and rare books inside his office. The book I wanted access to was located in a special area of the

Archive. Books on dark magic and entities of the night, as they were called, were forbidden to most. The knowledge was volatile, dangerous, and easily abused. Considering the current state of our relationship, there was a good chance I was going to get a violent 'no' on this one. I hoped Ronin was right.

I stood at the rune-covered door, took a deep breath, and knocked.

"Come in, Grey," a deep voice said.

The door whispered open, inviting me in.

My skin felt a slight burn as I walked past the threshold. "You've increased the defenses?" I asked, touching the exposed skin of my hand. It felt like a mild sunburn.

"Can never be too careful," Honor answered. "Knowledge is power, and power is always coveted."

"Good point," I said. "Better safe than crispy."

The last time we'd *conversed*, we had almost killed each other. I'd been angry. Blinded by betrayal and loss, I had come to him to find a way to reverse the dissolution…to save Jade.

I'd figured if anyone knew a way to reverse the spell, he would. He'd met me with the truth, I would discover later, and there was no undoing what I had done. I'd hated him. Blamed him for my mistake. Then I came to burn his books, convinced he was keeping the spell from me.

I bought into the unstoppable force meeting an immovable object paradox, thinking *I* was the unstoppable force. He'd stopped me…cold. Rather than shred me into small, stupid, mage parts, he'd banned me from the Central Archive, promising to kill me on sight if I ever stepped near the building.

"Indeed," he said. "Ronin said you found something for me."

I had to remember to thank Ronin for this…if I survived.

I stepped into the mid-sized office, pausing just inside the door. A large desk, carved from granite, dominated one side of the office. Sara Jay's voice softly filled the room over the deep bass of Massive Attack, as she seduced me with a story about a dissolved girl.

Honor's OCD was in high gear as I looked around the office. Every wall held cases filled with books. All of them were protected by an intricate network of runes and fail-safes. No one was getting to those books…alive, at least.

He was meticulous about order and organization. There were no books strewn about. "A place for everything, and everything in its place" was his mantra. Aside from the desk and the bookcases, his office was mostly empty space, except for some footstools to reach the higher shelves.

I walked over and placed Ziller's book on his desk, sliding it forward, and then stepped back. He never kept chairs for guests in his office. I remember asking him about that once. His response stayed with me to this day: *"No one stays in my office long enough to sit."*

I took another sip of my Deathwish as he narrowed his eyes at me and then looked down at the book. His eyes opened slightly, the only indication of surprise I would get.

He rested a finger on the cover. "Where did you get this book?"

"Ronin got it from Ziller," I said, opting for the truth. Honor had an uncanny bullshit detector. "Thought you should have it."

"His idea or yours?"

"After my last visit here, what do you think?"

ORLANDO A. SANCHEZ

"Yet, you still risked your life to bring it to me. Thank you for being honest."

Like I said, uncanny bullshit detector.

He put down the book he'd been holding and picked up Ziller's. In all the years we'd known each other, I'd never seen him without a book in his hand or in a pocket.

The same order and organization he applied to his office carried over into his appearance. Unlike most mages, who preferred suits, Honor leaned more toward the casual end of clothing. Jeans, a crisp black shirt with the sleeves rolled up, and work boots made up his ensemble. He had let his hair grow out since we last spoke, but he kept the beard as stubble. It was like looking at university professor Gandalf.

"Can you add that to your collection?"

His deep brown eyes bored into me as he placed the book gently on the table.

"When did you bond to it?"

"To what?"

"The blade keeping you among the living. You found a solution when I couldn't."

"Wasn't my solution," I said. "This was a gift from Hades."

"Hades?" he asked. "Gave you a bloodthirsty blade designed to undo supernatural entities? Why would he do that?"

"How did you know?"

"Kuro kokoro kokutan no ken," he said almost reverently, "is no ordinary sword. I can't believe Hades would give it to you."

"Me either," I said, "but here we are."

Honor shook his head. "If Ronin sent you, it must be dire. He knows our history."

"It is," I said, my voice grim. "I need help."

"Let me see the blade," he said. "I want to know how much damage you've done."

"Damage?" I asked. "What are you talking about?"

"You've bonded, which means it's part of you," he said. "Can you form it?"

I extended my arm, and formed Darkspirit. The blade glistened in the light as the red runes pulsed slowly.

Honor leaned back in his chair and stared at me.

I placed it in front of him, on the desk, but he refused to touch it.

"That's it," I said, looking down at Darkspirit. "Goes by the name of Izanami—goddess of destruction and creation. Usually chatty as hell, but she's quiet now."

"Shit, Grey," Honor said, almost breathless. "You don't know what you've done, do you?"

As long I had known him, I'd never really known how powerful he was. Some said he was stronger than an Archmage. All I knew was that the Dark Council, NYTF, and all of the sects left him alone to oversee the Archive. It wasn't because of his rugged good looks.

This was the first time I'd seen fear in his eyes.

SEVENTEEN

"What are you talking about?" I asked, trying to stomp on the fear that was brewing in my stomach. "It's just a sword."

"That"—he pointed at Darkspirit—"is not *just* a sword."

"True," I said. "It's also a colossal hemorrhoid, but other than that, it's a serviceable sword."

"I didn't know things were so bad. You should've come to me."

I took a deep breath. I didn't want this visit to go south, at least not before I got the information that I'd come for. I took another sip of Deathwish and counted to ten, making sure I got my breathing under control.

I extended my hand, absorbing Darkspirit.

"I did come to you, remember?" I made sure to keep the anger out of my voice. "You couldn't help me then."

"You were asking for the impossible," he said after a pause. "Entropic dissolutions can't be undone. Even now, the sword isn't undoing the damage, only preventing any further damage from occurring."

"It's keeping me alive," I said, clipping my words. "I knew this was a bad idea."

"No, no, listen, I don't want us to be enemies, Grey. You said you needed help. I take it it's with the creatures roaming the streets at night?"

"You ever hear of a 'Mr. Dark'?"

"Who gave you that name?"

"Ronin, and he says it could be one of Fluffy's names."

"Fluffy?"

"Long story. This creature masked an entire area of the park until I was surrounded by rummers, and then unleashed a rummogre on me."

"Did it exhibit control of the rummers and this…rummogre?"

"Yes, they were following its instructions, especially when it suggested they kill me."

Honor nodded, stood and stepped to one of his bookcases.

"Try to remember," he said, as he ran his finger along the spines of some of the books, "did it try to induce fear, or was it feeding on any fear already present? This is important."

I thought back to my encounter with Fluffy.

"It tried to induce fear first," I said. "Then it tried to find any fear I may have had. Neither worked."

He tapped his lip with a finger as he pulled out a book. "You're dealing with something old and dangerous," he said, looking up at me. "The creature you faced, if I'm correct, is called a Tenebrous."

"What is a Tenebrous?" I asked, never having heard the term before. "More importantly, how do I send it back to where it came from?"

He opened the book he'd pulled from the shelf, and placed it on the desk. Gesturing, he said some words under his breath, and the white lattice around the book fell away. As he turned the pages, I leaned forward, trying to read the text, then gave up since it was written in runes I couldn't decipher.

"What is that written in?"

"These are proto-runes," Honor answered. "Some of the first runes ever created."

"And you can read them?"

"Yes." He held up a finger as he turned pages. I didn't say anything else, as he had entered 'librarian researcher' mode. It was always this way when he studied something new or esoteric. The best thing was to let it run its course. "Here."

"I'm going to take your word for it."

He pointed to a section of the book.

"Says here they are the originators of pavormancy."

"Makes sense," I answered. "The whole 'fear me' thing was a dead giveaway."

"They inhabit dark mages, usually a pavormancer, but it can be any mage who operates by fear, inducing or harboring large amounts of fear."

"How do I stop it?" I asked. "Dispel the fear?"

"Close. You need to dispel the darkness."

"What? Shine a flashlight at it?" I asked. "Can you be any vaguer?"

"This is an old text. One second," he said. "Says here, you need to unleash a soulblaze. That is the only light that can destroy a Tenebrous. Do you know what a soulblaze is?"

"No," I said, but something was pulling at the back of my mind. "You said *inhabit*?"

"Yes, these creatures need a host," Honor said, tracing the book with his finger. "They will hunt mages and attempt to take over their bodies. If the mage is too weak, the victim is usually killed, dying a

93

horrible and terrifying death while facing their worst fears."

"This thing isn't *hunting* mages," I said. "It's house hunting, looking for somewhere to call home."

"That's an oversimplification, but yes, it's looking for a mage to reside in and control."

"Why didn't it work with me?"

"Your bond is probably the only thing that saved you when you faced it," Honor added. "It probed but found your sword had taken up residency. You were, in essence, occupied."

"I need to stop it before it settles in someone."

Honor shook his head. "I'm afraid I can't help you there. The text doesn't say anything more besides needing a soulblaze, whatever that is."

I strangled my knee-jerk reaction to ask if he was being straight with me, and took another breath.

"I thought you kept all the dangerous books in some other corner of the Archive?" I asked, glancing at the bookcases. "They all seem to be here."

"I used to, long ago, before a mage I knew smashed through my defenses, threatening to destroy some of them," he answered. "Now I keep them close."

"Wise move," I said, side-stepping the obvious reference to my younger, dumber, suicidal days. "I need two things." I held up two fingers. "Can you find out how these things are created or summoned?"

"I'd say summoned," Honor answered. "Tenebrous are ancient, according to this text. No one is going around *making* one of them. What's the second thing?"

"How do I find out about a soulblaze?"

"I'll look in our older texts, but this is one of the oldest," he said, pointing at the book he was reading. "If I were you, I'd try Aria."

"I'll head there next," I said. "Speaking of dangerous situations, I may need to go to Fordey Boutique. Are you still in contact with the Ten?"

"You want to stay away from Fordey for a few years," Honor answered, replacing the book on the shelf and then gesturing. A white lattice enveloped the spine. "They are dealing with some…situations."

"May not have a choice," I said. "I think they have a warden bag."

"Unkeyed?"

"I hope so. I don't want some dead warden's bag."

"If it's unkeyed, bring it to me," Honor replied. "I'll place failsafes to cope with your current sword *situation* and add a few texts of defensive magic."

"Thank you," I said, and meant it. "You know I never really apologized—"

"No need," he said. "Just don't try to destroy the Central Archive…ever again."

"Does this mean the KOS is lifted?"

"No," he said. "Rules must be upheld. You used violence within our walls. You are the only person alive who has done that and lived to talk about it. Consider yourself fortunate."

"Can it be modified?" I asked, not relishing the idea of Archivists out to erase me. I had enough people in the 'erase Grey' fan-club. "How about a proximity ban? I try to get into the Central Archive, feel free to ghost me?"

"Speaking of which," Honor began, "what made your cipher apprentice think she could get past our security? Doesn't she understand the concept of nothing being something?"

"I'm sure she does now," I said. "Proximity ban?"

"Actually, I'm considering enforcing it now," he said. "Take your apprentice and reduce your proximity to me—let's say to zero. If you need the

Central Archive, I'll have Rahbi place your apprentice on a provisional pass, provided she doesn't try her cipher ability again. You…I suggest *you* don't visit."

That was his way of saying yes, but I didn't want to push it. Having Honor as an enemy would make my life much shorter.

"Appreciate it," I said. "Is she still in stasis?"

He waved a hand. "She's free," he said. "Tell her if she tries to break in again, I won't be so nice next time. Next time, I take the fans."

"I'll let her know," I said, turning to leave.

"Grey," he said, his voice serious, "Darkspirit is lethal, not just to your targets, but to you too. We need to have a longer discussion when you aren't busy trying to save the city. In the meantime, try not to use it too often."

"That's what I have Fatebringer for," I said with a nod.

He nodded back. "Rahbi will see you out."

EIGHTEEN

Rahbi escorted us to the side door.

"You don't want to go out the front," she said. "Snipers—who may or may not observe the temporary suspension on the KOS."

"Thanks," I said. "I'll bring the Lockpick around when I've dealt with this craziness."

Rahbi glanced at a scowling and embarrassed Koda.

"She's not bad," Rahbi said, trying to cheer her up. "But our defenses are designed to stop *everything*. If you really want to learn how to get around security, come visit, and I'll show you a thing or two."

"Why would you do that?" I asked. "She's bad enough as it is."

"Yes," Rahbi said. "But she's not good enough yet, is she?"

Koda remained silent, but I could tell she enjoyed the idea of learning how to bypass security at a higher level.

"Please extend my thanks to Honor, again."

"Did you get everything you needed?" Rahbi asked, unlocking the door and standing in the doorway. "He seemed pleased about your gift."

"How do you know?"

"You're still breathing, aren't you?"

"Oh, good point."

"No one…I mean no one, has broken one of his rules like you have and lived to talk about it, Grey," she said. "Don't fuck this up…again."

"No intention of doing so, but I'm curious," I said, "aren't Ronin and Honor friends?"

"Depends on the context," Rahbi said, looking outside. "If you mean as two mages, then yes, Honor and Ronin are friends. If it has to do with Honor as an Archivist and the Central Archive, nothing and no one comes before the Archive."

"Ronin is dealing with the Magekiller."

"No, he isn't," Rahbi answered, her voice hard. "Division 13 is sanctioning his activities, despite his 'official' leave of absence. He still works for them, no matter how hard he pretends he doesn't."

"He's the reason I'm here," I said. "He provided the book for Honor."

"When you faced the creature earlier this evening," she started, "why didn't he step in to assist?"

"Good question," I said, understanding the implication of the surveillance. "If you had people there, why didn't you?"

"Because our people were there to finish you."

"What stopped you?"

"Let's just say not everyone hates Night Wardens."

"Honor didn't want D13 in here," I said, looking around.

"Unlike a certain dark mage, D13 is not a necessary evil. It's an organization that has repeatedly operated outside any established law and overstepped its bounds."

"Who watches the watchers?"

"Exactly," Rahbi answered. "In any case, they have their own concerns now, dealing with Tigris."

"Tigris? Like the river?"

"And so much more," she said, walking us to the Beast. "I think you need to be focused on the task at hand...hmm? Something about a Tenebrous? Dying mages?"

"Good point," I said, looking around. "Where's her ride?"

"We had the Shroud delivered to The Dive," Rahbi answered with a smile. "I didn't know how long you would be. Even camouflaged, it was going to be seen this close to the Central Archive."

"Cecil would be pissed if someone stole that bike."

"Indeed." Koda entered the passenger side in a silent funk. Rahbi stood outside my door as I settled in behind the wheel. "A word."

"Shoot."

"I hope I never have to."

"Me either," I answered. "I'd hate to make you miss."

She nodded and then raised a hand, made a fist and signaled to the left.

"Snipers?"

"Remember the Warden adage," she said. "Trust no one. I can guarantee you that whatever Ronin's involvement, it's not to help those dying mages. Tread carefully with him."

"Understood," I said, starting the Beast. "If he reaches out—"

"He won't," Rahbi said. "Somehow getting you and Honor together was—"

I sensed it a few seconds before it happened. I opened the door, grabbed Rahbi, and crushed the accelerator. The force of the explosion rocked the Beast from behind and nearly flipped us over. I was grateful the car had a fat ass loaded with armor plating. We skidded to a stop a few seconds later. A second explosion rocked the upper level of the Central Archive.

"Honor," Rahbi managed to say before jumping out of the Beast and running back to the now smoking Central Archive building.

"Holy hell," Koda said, snapping out of her funk. "Was that meant for us?"

I parked the Beast and ran back after Rahbi, with Koda on my heels.

"Eyes and ears open," I said, as we arrived at the edge of the Beast-sized crater we had left seconds earlier. "If Honor is dead, we'll be following him soon enough."

NINETEEN

We reached the top level of the Central Archive and headed for Honor's office. Even with the urgency of the moment, Rahbi had stopped in front of the office door and was methodically disabling the runes around the frame.

"Is that bad?" I asked. "I've never seen him lock that door while he's in the building."

"A little busy right now, Grey," Rahbi said under her breath as beads of sweat formed on her brow. "If I get these wrong, those two explosions won't even register compared to what would happen."

I looked around the smoking Central Archive. Most of the damage was contained to this floor, and specifically to this area of the floor. I drew Fatebringer just in case any Archivist thought this would be a good chance to get rid of a dark mage.

"How much of a hate mountain am I looking at right now?"

"Excuse me?" Rahbi said, still focusing on the door runes. "What are you talking about?"

"C'mon, Rahbi," I said, letting my senses expand, "dark mage gets a temporary suspension on a KOS, visits Honor, and then a few minutes after the dark mage leaves, the Central Archive explodes?"

"Shit, that does look bad," Koda added. "It was a setup."

"No shit. Now the dark mage and *his apprentice*, who tried to breach Central Archive's security, I might add—"

"Sorry?" Koda said, looking away. "I still don't know how they saw me."

"Looks like they tried to take out a threat on their lives," I continued, ignoring her apology. "Like I said, how much hate is coming my way?"

"The Light Council already thinks you're way past being retired," Rahbi said, working the last of the runes. "It all depends on how much damage was done."

I shook my head. "Not for them it won't."

She unlocked the final rune and opened the door. It was a surreal image. The center of the office looked like it had been used for artillery practice. Parts of the floor were scorched or missing. Now I understood why Honor kept his office so spartan. All of the shelves holding books glowed with a bright orange light. Not one book in them was damaged.

In the center of the destruction, under a pulsing, violet semi-circle of power, lay an unconscious Honor. In his hand, he held the tattered remains of Ziller's book. He looked banged up. Parts of his shirt and jeans were smoldering, and he had gotten himself one killer of a tan. The first-degree burns he was showing meant he deflected most of the explosion. He was alive, but he would need medical attention.

"That was the book I gave him."

"Grey," Rahbi said, her soft voice a scythe cutting

through the commotion starting outside, "tell me you didn't have anything to do with this."

"I would never do anything to deliberately hurt Honor, or the Archive."

"That book incriminates you"—she glanced at Koda—"and her failed security breach incriminates her. They'll come for both of you."

"Shit," I said, feeling the start of a massive headache forming behind my eyes. "We didn't do this, but you'd better believe I'm going find out who did."

"I believe you," she said, staring at me hard. "But you'd better leave. This looks exactly like what it's supposed to look like."

"It's a setup."

"Not to the Light Council," she said. "To them, it will look like you lost your mind—what little you have left, attacked Honor and the Archive in some vendetta scenario."

"Someone benefits from having him out of play," I said, remembering the blast under the Beast. "It was supposed to be both of us. Someone miscalculated."

She nodded. "The sphere around him is a personal failsafe. I won't be able to disable it for at least an hour."

"What about his condition? He needs medical attention. Those burns look serious."

"I'm a trained medic. Every Archive has one. I can keep him stable until the sphere dissipates. You two need to get scarce, now. The Light Council will be on the scene within the hour."

"I'll find out who did this," I said, heading for the door. I looked at Koda and motioned with my head for her to get moving. "This won't go unanswered. Not on my watch."

"You'd better find them before I do," Rahbi said,

ORLANDO A. SANCHEZ

moving closer to the violet sphere. "You may want to ask Ronin some questions. Starting with, why the book he gave you exploded?"

We moved quickly out of Dragonflies before the Light Council arrived with thoughts of having lethal conversations and erasing dark mages and their apprentices.

TWENTY

We jumped into the Beast and sped off.

"You really think that Ronin guy did this?" Koda asked.

I had too many thoughts racing in my head to straighten them out. I needed a near-lethal dose of Deathwish if I was going to make sense of this. The throbbing had reached samba level and was edging into a drum and bass beat, with my head as the drum.

"I need coffee," I said with a groan, pinching the bridge of my nose. "Just enough to deal with the drumline from hell in my skull."

"You just had coffee," Koda said. "Isn't that what you were drinking back there?"

"No one makes coffee like Cole," I answered. "Besides, we need to get your bike."

"Right," she said, and I could sense her shutting down. Better to rip this one off like a bandage.

"What happened?" I asked. "I thought you were invisible, being a cipher and all?"

"I don't know. One moment I'm bypassing the door runes, the next I'm looking up into that lady's face."

"That *lady*...is Rahbi," I said. "Consider yourself

lucky to be in one piece. If there is anyone worthy of respect and lots of space, it's her."

"Can you take her?"

"Where to? Lunch? Dinner?"

"You know what I mean," Koda said. "Can you beat her?"

"Every person you meet is a not a potential enemy."

"Hasn't been my experience," she said. "Treat everyone like an enemy, then you won't be disappointed when they stab you in the back."

"That's a shitty outlook on life and people."

"Says Mr. 'Trust-no-one.' Sure, I'll get right on the Grey Stryder system of 'How to Make Friends in Ten Lethal Steps.'"

"I didn't say you needed to make friends—"

"Step One," she continued. I braced myself to let the rant run its course. "Find a friend with a large home or business and proceed to destroy it. Preferably in an explosive and spectacular way. Show them you really care by blasting it to bits."

"That's not what happened here," I said, "and you know it. I think you have me confused with another mage that roams this city."

"Step Two...oh, wait, no other steps needed," Koda said, holding up two fingers. "After step one, everyone is out to erase your ass. Good job."

"Listen, you don't get to be an old, beat-up, cynical warden until you fulfill the first two," I said. "Old and beat-up, not young and entitled."

"Entitled?" she shot back. "Do you even know how Hades trains his assassins?"

"No," I said. "I just know about the ones who botch jobs or fail the training. None of them are around to piss and moan about their life. Seems like Hades has a killer retirement plan."

Silence and a nod.

"Thought so," I said. "Stop your bitching and put that brain of yours to work. We have a world of pain headed our way. What have you learned?"

"You are really cranky without coffee, wow."

"I meant regarding our current situation, smartass," I snapped, swerving around traffic, "not my general demeanor. Now, break it down."

"Fine. Someone is flooding the streets with a new strain of Redrum."

"Redrum X. Finding that supplier is our priority, why?"

"Because whoever it is, they're targeting the homeless population."

"Yes, and what else?"

"Whatever is out there is using the rummers to attack or hunt down mages," she answered. "Even though the reason is unclear."

"The reason is clearer now."

"It is?" she asked. "You mean you know why rummers are being made?"

"No, that's why I was pursuing the Haran lead Aria gave me."

"Have you located him?"

"No. Not yet, but I have a lead on where to find him."

"Let me guess," she said. "Some deep underground lair full of insane ex-Wordweavers, ready to shred us."

"No. I have to check with the Exiles. Which can be just as bad as a lair of deranged Wordweavers."

"Aria said he was an Exile who left them several years ago."

"That was the lead I was tracking when Street called."

"Why are mages being hunted?"

"They aren't being hunted," I said. "The creature that's out there killing them, is called a Tenebrous."

"Darkness?" Koda asked. "Kind of fits."

"According to Ronin, it goes by 'Mr. Dark.' Tried to scare me shitless before it attacked me," I said. "It uses fear and then tries to take over the body. It's targeting mages for power."

"Mr. Dark...did you come up with this name?"

"No, I call it Fluffy." I couldn't help the smile. "Pisses it right off."

"I think I prefer Fluffy to the cliché....really."

"That's what Ronin called it," I said. "I wonder how long he's been tracking it. That body Street found wasn't the first."

"I doubt it'll be the last," she said. "And it didn't scare you because...?"

"I don't scare that easily, but more importantly, I'm occupied."

"What?" she asked. "You're busy?"

"I'm *bonded* to the sword," I said. "I have enough darkness inside me for a several mages."

"And then some," Koda said. "Fluffy probably looked in you and said: *Damn, that's dark. No room for me.*"

"Also because I was strong enough to resist the initial attack," I said, shaking my head. "It's looking for power in a weak mind. The mage's body has to be strong enough to withstand being taken over. This isn't some low-level creature."

"But the mind has to be weak?"

"Something like that," I answered. "I wouldn't say weak, more like malleable."

"I wonder if the bond to my fans makes me immune?"

"I'd rather not have to find out," I said. "Call Cole and tell him I need about a gallon of Deathwish."

"Don't you think you drink too much—?"

"If that sentence is going to end with 'coffee,' I recommend you stop now," I said with a growl. "Coffee is good for your health."

"My health? Since when?"

"Since my drinking it squashes my headaches, allowing me to stay stable, therefore not lashing out in anger, and erasing those near and dear to me. See how that works? Good for *your* health."

She connected a call to The Dive, while I reached out to Aria.

"Aria," I said, as my comm made the call.

She picked up after the third ring.

"Hello, Grey," she said. "Was that you at the Archives?"

"I was there," I said. "But it wasn't me."

"You'd better get here as soon as possible."

The urgency in her voice was unfamiliar. Aria didn't spook easily. If something had her worried, that meant I needed to be petrified.

But, like I told Koda, I didn't scare easily.

TWENTY-ONE

"I'm heading to The Dive, and then I'm on my way."

"That would be unwise," Aria answered. "Your bar is being watched by the Light Council."

"When you say *watched*, do you mean—?"

"Currently, a group of mages and shifters are tasked with eliminating you or your apprentice, the moment either of you approach the property."

I glanced at Koda and shook my head. She ended her call as I raced across town. We were headed to the Cloisters.

"They'd better not touch Cole, Frank, or The Dive."

"I informed them that moving on anyone outside of the kill order would be most unwise," she said. "They agreed to leave the bar and your associates alone. You and your apprentice are another matter entirely."

"So straight-up elimination?" I asked. "What? No conversation? No, 'Hey, why did you blow up the Archive'? Just shoot first?"

"The Light Council is not the Dark Council, Grey," she said. "The mages will hate you on principle for going dark."

"Hypocrites," I said. "Like they haven't thought of casting a dark spell."

"Thinking is not doing," she answered with a sigh. "The shifters still remember the Wardens from the Purge. It wasn't a good time."

"And the Archivists?"

"Did you blow up the Archive?" Aria asked, her voice betraying no emotion. "They, although they rarely leave their archives, are considering forming a task force just for you."

"Now I feel special. They're willing to leave their dank and dusty libraries just to come and hunt me?"

"Archivists are accomplished mages, some of them much stronger than you."

"And now they want to come out and play?"

"I have to say, you bring out a special kind of rage in people. And you didn't answer my question."

If she was asking, this situation had just gone from bad to apocalyptic.

"How bad is it?"

"The Light Council asked us to intervene on their behalf."

"What did you say?"

"I told them I needed to speak to you first."

I let the words hang for a few seconds. This was making 'apocalyptic' look like a vacation destination.

"I didn't blow up the damn Archive or Honor," I said, frustrated. "Why would I go through all that trouble? They already have a KOS on me, so what's it going to be now? KOS Plus Ultra? Now they're going to unleash all their might to move against me?"

"Tell me what happened."

I explained the situation as best as I could to her.

"It was the book Ronin gave me that exploded. Which makes it look bad."

"Things are not always what they appear to be, Grey," she replied. "You of all people know this."

"Well, this looks like I went to the Archive to blow it, and Honor, up."

"There are some more questions I need answered," she said. "But I will wait until you arrive. Disable all defensive runes on your vehicle. You and your apprentice will need to surrender your weapons upon entry."

"Really, do the Wordweavers think I'm going to go from blowing up the Central Archive to storming the Cloisters? I'm insane, not suicidal."

"It's a lockdown protocol, and you *will* abide by it," she said, her voice making sure it wasn't a request. "I may lead these Wordweavers, but I'm not a dictator."

"Of course I'll abide by it," I said. "Last thing I need is a bunch of angry Wordweavers after me."

"This book…tell me about it," she asked. "And tell me what he said exactly, in regards to getting information on the Tenebrous."

"You know what it is?"

I could feel she was giving me a look like 'you can't possibly be this dense'.

"I meant—you know what it is."

"Yes, I do, even though there hasn't been one in this area since the war."

"Well, this one can control rummers, make rummogres, and has some serious masking ability," I said. "Oh, and it likes its targets scared—as in terrorized."

"They thrive on fear," she said. "What did Ronin say regarding the book and its delivery?"

I took a moment to avoid smearing a yellow cab and raced on to the West Side Highway, heading uptown. I tried to remember what Ronin had said about getting the book to Dragonflies, and Honor.

"He wanted information on the Tenebrous," I said. "I informed him you wouldn't let him near your library, at least not while he was breathing."

"Close," she said. "Division 13 and its operatives are not welcome within the Cloisters' walls or surrounding property."

"That's when he suggested Honor and Dragonflies."

"He suggested it? Not you? Think, Grey, this is important."

"I would never suggest Honor or the Dragonflies. We weren't on speaking terms. The last thing I would do is send Ronin, or anyone, to the Central Archives."

"Is that when he suggested giving Honor the book?"

"He mentioned he didn't have the access a dark mage does, then pushed the book on me, as a way to smooth over what happened between Honor and me."

"The book was a ruse and you walked into a trap."

"You think?" I asked. "I'll be there in ten minutes. We can discuss the rest then."

"Remember what I said about the defensive runes and weapons."

"Got it," I said. "No defensive runes on the Beast, and we hand over our weapons."

"Exactly, Grey," she said. "Remember your favorite saying."

"I never forget it."

"See you soon," she added. "Oh, and don't forget to get rid of that old rag of a coat. Wear something appropriate for once."

"The old duster is getting a bit ragged around the edges."

"You should really get yourself a new one, that

one looks like it's been stomped on by several ogres
—at once."

She ended the call. I got off the Henry Hudson
Parkway and drove into Fort Washington Park,
stopping at the Point, under the George Washington
Bridge.

"Shit."

"What is it?" Koda asked. "Why did you stop?
Where are we?"

"You heard half the conversation," I said,
motioning for her to get out as I opened the door.
"Extrapolate."

"It sounded like she wanted you to disarm the
Beast," Koda started, "and that we're supposed to
hand over our weapons? Is that right?"

"She called my duster an 'old rag of a coat' right
before she hung up."

"Didn't she make that coat for you?"

I nodded. "That sound like Aria to you?"

"No, she'd never say that about your duster or our
weapons. Since when do we ever disarm the Beast?
What's going on?"

"Light Council must be parked in the Cloisters," I
said, moving to the rear of the Beast and opening the
trunk. "C'mere."

I handed her a pack. "What's this?" she asked,
hefting it in her hand. "A present? You shouldn't
have."

"I didn't. Go in the back of the Beast and change,"
I said, taking off my duster and placing it on the
ground. "Make it fast."

She jumped in the Beast as I reached in the trunk
for another pack similar to the one I'd given her. Soft
runes glowed orange as I opened it.

"These are backup leathers?" she yelled from

inside the Beast. "I thought you said you only had one set made up?"

"Less talking, more moving," I said, removing an identical brown duster from the pack. "Hand me the ones you were wearing."

In actuality, I'd had several sets of leathers made for her. The same way I had several dusters located throughout the city and in The Dive, in addition to the spare I kept in the Beast.

She handed me the leathers she'd had on. I placed them on the ground next to my duster. This part was going to hurt.

Koda stepped out of the Beast.

"Care to share what we're doing?"

"Someone wants us out of the way," I said, and gritted my teeth against the oncoming pain. "You're going to want to get back in the Beast."

"Seriously?"

"Only if you want to keep breathing."

"I like breathing."

"Beast, now then," I said, pointing to the car. "This will take a few minutes, then I'll explain."

Aria had just let me know we were heading into a trap.

TWENTY-TWO

I formed Izanami and began the spell.

<Are you certain you want to do this...here?>

"Not much of a choice," I said, taking a deep breath. "Someone on the Light Council is playing dirty and using Division 13 to set me up."

<Flowing water will mean you need to use more power than usual. You will experience considerable pain.>

I looked over at the Hudson River. Above us sat the George Washington Bridge, leading into Jersey. Farther north, past the bridge, sat Fort Tryon Park and the Cloisters. Around me, I could swear I smelled the slightest hint of cinnamon.

"I know. My entire life has been pain. We're good friends."

<Understood. What do you need from me?>

"I need you to plant a beacon simulating the tracking spell on these items. Can you do it?"

<You mean a rudimentary spell of mimicry?>

"That's what I just said. Yes or no?"

<You realize I'm a goddess?>

"So you keep reminding me," I said, taking a deep breath. "Can you do it? Dawn will be in a few hours, and I don't intend on being here at sunup."

<Of course I can do it.> Izanami scoffed. <Honestly, I don't know what's more insulting, the request or the question asking if I can fulfill it.>

"I'm not questioning your godly powers, but we're pressed for time. I figure once they notice we haven't moved, they'll come for us."

<I advise less speaking and more casting.>

I glared at the blade.

Of course I'd get a dark blade with a snippy goddess. Why couldn't I get a not-so-dark blade with a laid-back goddess? One who felt an afternoon of eliminating beers was an afternoon well spent? No, I had to get the blade with a goddess who had an ego the size of the city.

I walked several meters away with the clothing and plunged the blade into the ground, next to the pile. The runes in the clothing immediately flared orange.

<Again with the burying me in the ground. I'm a refined weapon of death, and you only see fit to bury me in the ground. Maybe you should bond to a shovel?>

"If the shovel didn't speak, then, yes, I would bond to it," I said, gesturing. "At least it would be quieter in my head."

I whispered the spell and gestured. Black energy erupted around me, followed by the sensation of a hot knife plunging into my skull. I nearly screamed at the searing pain. Being this close to the river meant I needed about twice as much energy to cast this spell. Double the energy, double the excruciating fun.

The area around the clothing turned black and began consuming the materials. A black cloud of lethal mist filled with glowing red runes floated up from the ground, remaining in place, immune to the gentle wind. It would expand for a few more meters and then set off a runic beacon.

<You may have made it too strong.>

"I had to compensate for the river."

<It will attract the creature and many others. Was that your goal?>

"How many others?"

<I do not keep a census of creatures in this city. Judging from the strength of the spell...many others.>

I let my senses expand for a few seconds. Nothing triggered my radar.

"I'm not sensing anything. You sure you aren't overreacting?"

<I am a goddess. I do not overreact.>

"What you are is a pain in my ass," I said. "I just need to get Fluffy here while I take care of some things downtown."

I absorbed Darkspirit.

The spell served several purposes. One was to create the impression that we were at this location. In order to do that, I needed to use items that were immersed in our energy signatures. My duster and her leathers were ideal for this spell, but they were also the fuel for the process.

I was going to have to make some serious apologies to Aria later for destroying them. I knew a spell of undoing this advanced would distress Aria considerably. She prided herself in having her garments being nearly indestructible. One of the things I learned early on: Every spell has a counter. It all depends on if you're willing to pay the cost.

The reason for the spell was to get Fluffy's attention and bring it to this location. I was going downtown and preferred the creature going in the opposite direction.

If it was hunting mages, this spell was like setting a plate of the finest food in front of a starving man. I only hoped we were close enough for it to sense the energy signature from the Wordweavers. I closed my eyes and let my senses expand. The Cloisters lit up on my radar without trying. We were close enough.

I didn't want the Light Council to feel cheated when we didn't show up.

If I got this wrong, Aria was going to be incredibly pissed. If I got it right, the Tenebrous would head north and crash into the Cloister's defenses, keeping the Wordweavers busy at least until dawn, and hopefully removing enough of the Light Council from the property that I could pay Aria a visit later without having to fight for my life. Either way, we were headed in a different direction for the time being.

"Let's go," I said to the camouflaged Koda as she materialized next to me. "We need to get scarce before Fluffy gets here."

"How did you see me?" Koda asked, angry. "What the hell?"

She stomped ahead of me to the Beast.

"Maybe you're losing your ability."

She stopped walking as I headed back to the Beast, passing her.

"That's not even a little funny, old man," she said, pointing at me.

"I don't know"—I shook my head—"first the Archive stops you cold, now here out in the open. What good is a camouflage if everyone can see you? Seems more like cannot-flage."

"You didn't know I was there," she said after a pause. "There's no way you knew."

She was right, of course. I just took a guess, knowing her nature to defy direct orders. I was about to answer when I felt the chill. Behind us, I felt the familiar presence.

"Hello, Grey."

"Oh, shit," I said, turning slowly. "Seems like I miscalculated the strength of the spell."

<I told you.>

"You called?"

"I did," I said, backing up slowly. "Koda, you want to get close to the Beast."

It was a young mage this time. Younger than the broken one in the park. He was dressed in torn jeans and an old leather jacket. His hair was a mess, and his face was covered in bruises. It was the eyes that convinced me, though. There must have been a small part of the mage left, and that infinitesimal trace of the mage's mind was screaming in sheer terror.

He turned in a circle, arms outstretched, and laughed.

"How do I look?" the mage asked, looking down at his body. "He's not strong and won't last long, but I couldn't resist when you called me so powerfully."

"Grey, what the fuck?" Koda hissed. "Who…what is that?"

"Where *are* my manners?" the mage said with a bow. "My apologies. Would you like me to make the introductions?"

Behind the young mage, I sensed them. Rummers, and something more.

Something worse.

TWENTY-THREE

"Hello again, Grey. It really has been too long."

"Not long enough," I muttered under my breath.

"Grey," Koda said, and I could hear the fear as her eyes glazed over. "I'm scared. The walls, they're closing in."

"And it's delicious," Fluffy said. "You didn't tell me you had such a meal, Grey."

"Koda," I said. "Koda! Is that how you're going out? You're going to let some piece of shit creature scare you to death?"

Some of the light came back to her eyes, and she focused. Her hands were trembling, but it wasn't from fear.

"What…the…royal fuck?" she yelled at the mage, materializing her fans. "You tried to get in my head? No one…gets in my head…and lives."

"I *did* get in," Fluffy said. "So much fear. You're like a ten-course meal. I'm going to take my time with you. Do you mind, Grey?"

"First of all," I said, "stop calling me Grey like we're friends. It's 'Night Warden' or 'Mr. Night

Warden.' And, secondly, do I know you? The face doesn't seem familiar. When did we meet?"

I needed to push his buttons. Get him off-balance.

"You've forgotten me so soon?" Fluffy said, motioning with his hand. "Let me refresh your memory."

Two rummogres appeared next to him. Each rummogre was accompanied by twenty rummers. The foghorn of doom reverberated in my head. This was going to be bad.

I may have pushed the button too hard.

"Oh, I think it's coming back now," I said, drawing Fatebringer and forming Darkspirit. "Is that you, Fluffy?"

"I'm going to enjoy breaking you, Warden. You're going to watch as I make your little friend beg for her death."

I saw the hatred behind the mages's eyes. I knew it wasn't just the name, something deeper was going on here, but I was going to milk the name for all its worth. Because I was considerate like that.

I narrowed my eyes, looking at the mage. A cloud of runically charged darkness enveloped him. The Tenebrous was redlining his body and burning him out. The mage didn't have long before he ended up broken and dead.

From where I stood, I could see the dark liquid trickle down one nostril. Blood.

"Fluffy, that mage isn't strong enough to contain you. Let him go."

"Seems like my time is almost up," Fluffy said, wiping his nose. "Mages, they just don't make them like they used to."

"Release him."

"He's already gone. Once I occupy a body, the mind is broken beyond repair," Fluffy answered with a smile. "But don't worry, right after I kill you, I was thinking of a new home."

"A new home?" I said, stepping closer. "I know an awesome gerbil you can use as a host."

"Your attempts at goading me won't work, Grey."

"I told you, don't call me—touché."

Mages—always a touchy bunch. He gave me a slight nod.

"Gerbil? No, I don't think so. I was thinking another mage. Someone a little stronger than this"—he pointed to his body—"shell. Someone like a deranged mage you may know. Does the name Street ring a bell?"

"You're going to have to kill me first," I said, firing Fatebringer.

Fluffy cast a shield and rolled to the side, avoiding my rounds.

"That's the plan," he said, casting another shield. The rummogres closed in on him and blocked any frontal attack with their bodies. He was using them as shields.

I holstered Fatebringer and closed on him. From my earlier experience, taking out the host wouldn't affect the rummogres or rummers, but having one less enemy to deal with made sense. I didn't want to kill the mage, despite what Fluffy said about him being already gone. Maybe Rox could help him if we got him to Haven in time.

Time…it was the one thing we were running out of. Every second the Tenebrous spent inside his body, he was doing damage. I needed a fast solution to deal with the mage. Preferably one that didn't kill me.

Koda had closed the distance on the rummers with a yell. Forty rummers, two rummogres and one monstrously inhabited mage. The odds seemed slightly against us.

125

<I can assist, unless—of course—you have 'this situation under control' as you usually do.>

Somehow I knew I was going to regret this. *<I need to take out the mage...fast.>*

<Take out? Do you mean eliminate?>

<No..take out as in neutrali—as in remove. We need him unconscious, but alive.>

<Cut him. I will do the rest.>

<Is that all? I just need to cut him?>

<So simple, even you can understand it.>

<You don't have a sense of humor, but you seem to have mastered sarcasm.>

Fluffy fired several small, black orbs my way. I deflected one, sliced through another and let my duster take the third. The impact lifted me off my feet, launching me back several meters. I landed hard and slid for a few meters more, coming to a stop with a grunt.

"Ow," I muttered, standing unsteadily. "That wasn't fun. Can we not do that again?"

"Duck!" Koda yelled. I dropped to the ground as a fan sliced through the air above me, removing two rummers closing in on my location. "Graceful as a brick, old man."

I drew Fatebringer and dropped two more rummers. The rummogres remained next to Fluffy, like enormous bodyguards. Four more rummers burst into dust around us as Koda's anger transformed itself into a lethal fan dance of death.

<Izanami, I hope you know what you're doing.>

<At least one of us does. Go cut him. I will deal with the threat.>

I formed several orbs. The casting squeezed the back of my neck like a vise as I unleashed them. The orbs whirled rapidly, moving in tandem, cutting through the groups of rummers and dispatching them. In the commotion, I ran at the mage.

The rummogres mobilized to intercept me. The pain from the casting threatened to knock me off my feet. The lack of caffeine in my system was becoming a liability.

I managed to dodge one enormous fist and slid around a life-ending stomp as I closed in on Fluffy.

"Stop him!" Fluffy yelled as he backpedaled, casting another spell. "Kill him!"

The mage was bleeding from his eyes and I knew this host was almost done. I closed the distance and sliced his arm at the shoulder, turning as I cut and slid right into a massive rummogre fist. New levels of pain flooded my body as I became airborne again.

<Such darkness. We will use this, mage.>

I sailed across the grass. A tree graciously refused to move for me, stopping my flight with bone-jarring force. I slammed into it back-first, sliding to the ground and ending up on my back. I groaned as I realized my everything hurt. If I survived this night, I'd have a talk with Aria about creating an anesthetic rune for the duster.

I stared up at the night sky. It was moments like these when you analyzed and questioned your life choices. Clearly, I had made some dubious ones to get me to this point. Maybe it *was* time for me to retire.

"Grey! Move, old man!" Koda yelled in my direction. "Get out of the way!"

The urgency in her voice, coupled with the micro-tremors I felt, must have been the rummogres closing in on me to complete the retirement-squashing ceremony. That's when the power flooded my body.

<Stand up, mage.>

127

TWENTY-FOUR

I rose to my feet effortlessly as energy thrummed through Darkspirit in my hand. It felt like holding a large tuning fork that had just been struck.

Black tendrils of power raced around my body as the rummogres closed on my position. All the pain was gone. The only thing I felt was power, rage…and darkness.

Sweet darkness.

The first rummogre closed in and swung a fist designed to remove my head. I ducked under the fist and swung Darkspirit, removing the arm at the shoulder. The rummogre howled in pain, its screams filling the night. I walked toward Fluffy.

The second rummogre rushed at my position in a football tackle. I raised the blade overhead, letting the power coalesce, and stood my ground. When the rummogre was two meters away, I sliced downward, bisecting the creature with a dark scythe of energy.

I kept walking toward Fluffy, who was now desperately casting what I could only assume was a nasty Warden disintegration spell. He flung several orbs as he kept casting. I deflected them with ease.

The host body was bleeding profusely now. His eyes, ears, nose, and mouth were covered in blood.

I formed a black orb as I closed the distance.

Fluffy released his casting—a dark spell of obliteration. I let Darkspirit absorb it.

"Impossible," Fluffy said. "You…you should be dead."

"I said release him." I unleashed the orb I held—an energy shunt. "Now."

It hit Fluffy in the chest and jettisoned the dark energy from the mages's destroyed body. The first rummogre ran at me from behind. When you're large enough to make the earth shake on your approach, frontal attacks are usually your best bet. I flung Darkspirit behind me, impaling the rummogre in the chest, and stopping it in its tracks. A second later, it burst into dust with a groan.

"This vessel was weak, Warden," Fluffy said into the night, "but I will find the right host and destroy you, your apprentice, and everything you treasure."

I looked into the night and unleashed the darkness within. I felt it fill the space around me.

"I don't know what you really are, and I don't know what you want. What I do know is that I have a very particular set of skills—skills I have acquired over two centuries as a Night Warden. This makes me a nightmare for creatures like you. If you don't return to where you came from, I *will* look for you, I *will* find you, and I *will* destroy you."

Laughter echoed through the night.

"Good luck, Warden," Fluffy replied, its voice growing fainter. "I will see you again, soon."

Koda approached, and I stared at her impassively. The darkness had me in its grip, and I was reluctant to let go. I knew the moment I did, the pain would return.

"Grey?" she said, waving a hand. "You in there? Is your brain taken?"

I looked around at the piles of dust that would be gone by sunrise. That's all humans were...dust, powerless, deserving to be ruled and controlled. I shook my head.

"Hell no," I said, gritting my teeth. "We will not be going on any power trips today."

I absorbed Darkspirit and released the remaining dark energy. The pain embraced me immediately, making me gasp and fall to my knees. I then staggered back to my feet.

<Don't do that again—ever.>

<Do what? I was merely making an observation.>

<I know what you were doing. You try putting thoughts in my head again, we're done. Even if it means I have to check out.>

<Like I said, merely an observation.>

<Refrain from those kinds of observations from now on. Understood?>

<Of course.>

I didn't trust her. I needed to find a solution to this sword situation before I really did go on a dark mage rampage and try to take over the world.

"That you, old man? Or am I dealing with the psychosword?"

"Of course it's me," I growled. "If you were dealing with the sword, I would have sliced you to pieces by now."

"Good to know," Koda said with a shudder. "Welcome back. You look like ogre-stomped shit."

"Thanks," I said. "You're not looking so great yourself."

"Yes, but I have an excuse. I was fighting overwhelming numbers. You only fought three creatures,"—she held up three fingers—"two

131

industrial sized ogre-rummer things and one wasted mage."

"I seem to remember taking out some of those rummers."

She propped me up by one shoulder as we walked to the Beast.

"And you clearly suffered some head trauma. I saw you bounce off that tree, the ground, the big ogre's fist and the—"

"I get it," I said, interrupting her. "I got my ass kicked."

"Ass kicked? Oh no, this was an O.S.B.D.—old school beatdown."

"Look at that, learn something new every day," I said. "Can you stop talking now? Even my thoughts hurt."

"Should I call Haven?"

"Haven," I said, remembering suddenly. "I need to speak to Roxanne. That thing is going after Street."

I placed the call and patched it through my connector.

"Grey?" Rox's voice came over the comms. "Where are you?"

"Where's Street?" I asked, ignoring her question. "Tell me he's still there."

"We released him an hour ago," she said. "I had no reason to hold him. You know how he gets if he's kept in here too long."

"Can you trace him?"

"No, why would I need to do that?" she asked. "I mean, given enough time I probably could. Tell me what's going on. Is he in danger?"

"Later. Right now I need to find Street. Wait, can you trace my beacon?"

There was a pause. "Yes, faintly, but yes, near the bridge."

"There's a body here, a young mage who was used and then killed. Can you have your team pick him up?"

"Yes, did you—?"

"No," I said. "The Tenebrous killed him. Burned right through his body."

"Grey, you sound terrible," she said, sounding concerned. "Why don't you come see me and recuperate from whatever it is you're doing?"

If I agreed to that, she'd have me in a bed for days. I knew Rox meant well, but she took the mothering thing too seriously. I wasn't insane enough to tell her that to her face, though. She was still an insanely powerful sorceress.

"Right after I'm done." Or dead. "I need to find Street, which means I need Frank."

"I'll have my morgue team pick up the mage. Call me when you can."

"I will, promise."

I ended the call and dialed The Dive on the regular line. If the Light Council was watching The Dive, they wouldn't expect a call on this line. They'd expect a call on my private line.

"You've reached The Dive, where no one knows your name or cares. Cole speaking."

"I need the lizard, now," I said and hung up.

TWENTY-FIVE

A few minutes after my call, an arc of electric energy hit the ground near us. This was quickly followed by a thunder clap and the pungent smell of chlorine. A string of curses that would make a sailor blush could be heard throughout the park.

"How does something so small curse so immensely?"

"I'm bigger on the inside," Frank retorted, orienting himself. Next to him, on the ground, was a large thermos. "Do not underestimate little things. Atoms are small things, until you split one. Now, stop bitching. I'm here, aren't I? By the way, Cole sent Deathwish—you're welcome."

"I think you just saved the city," Koda said, as I grabbed the thermos and drank deeply from the warm javambrosia. "He's been at maximum crankyass for a few hours now."

"Took you long enough," I said, sipping more Deathwish as Frank approached. "You take the scenic route?"

"The Dive is crawling with Light Council. How did you manage to piss them off? I thought you were already persona non grata with them after your

Fahrenheit 451 move at Dragonflies after, you know…?"

"I know," I said, not wanting to get into it. "Still am, this is just the seasoning on the KOS order."

"Oh, I understand, you're going for a record to see how many of these groups you can effectively piss off in one lifetime. Got it."

"It's my special warden skill. Listen, we have a situation."

"What the hell are you doing way the hell out here?" Frank said, looking around and then paused. "Holy hell, you look like you should be in Haven—for at least a month or two. Ugh, Lockpick too. Have you two taken up underground fighting? What gives?"

"Hey, *my* bruises will heal," Koda fired back. "Tomorrow, you'll still be a *lizard*."

"Enough, we don't have time for this," I said. "Frank, no BS, I need you to locate Street, now."

He must've heard the tone in my voice, because he grew serious and flicked his tail.

"Move back…now," he said and turned in a circle. "What fresh hell have you unleashed now, Grey?"

"I didn't unleash it, but I'm sure as hell going to put it down," I said. "Did you find him?"

"Did you lose him?"

"Not exactly. He was at Haven, Rox just discharged him about an hour ago."

"Okay, that helps…now, shut up and let me work."

I stepped back and leaned on the Beast. I had a severe case of B3—battered, bruised, and beaten. The only reason I was still in one piece was because of my duster. I was sure Koda could say the same thing about her leathers.

"You think he'll find him in time?" she asked.

I nodded. "It's not the finding I'm worried about,"

I said under my breath. "What do we do after Frank locates him?"

"What do you mean?" Koda asked, resting next to me against the Beast. "We keep him safe."

"Street may be mentally challenged, but he's a powerful mage. I'm not looking forward to fighting him on a regular day, much less one where he's being controlled by Fluffy."

"Shit," Koda said. "He won't stay at Haven. Is there anywhere else?"

I looked north, past the bridge. "Yes, but he isn't going to like it."

"Aria?"

I nodded.

"If I can get him behind the Cloister walls, she can keep him safe until we deal with this threat."

"Why does this sound near impossible?"

"Because it is, "I said. "I think I have a way to get him there, but I'm going to need the equivalent of chocolate gold...the good stuff."

"Hershey's?" Koda asked, confused. "Why are we discussing chocolate like it's drugs?"

"No, not Hershey's...Knipschildt—Madeline au Truffle, about two pounds. And for these beings, chocolate is better than drugs or money. They won't take anything else."

"You're serious?" Koda asked in disbelief. "You're going to pay for something with chocolate?"

"This isn't just chocolate, this is an experience," I answered. "I think I still have some in stasis. Just need to check my duster. This would be a perfect time for a warden bag."

"I found him," Frank said. "Bastard is moving around so fast I can't get a lock. Grand Central Terminal is where I sense him."

"Why would he be moving around fast?" Koda asked.

"Good question," I said. "Can you track what level he's on?"

"You do realize Grand Central is immense? And we're—where the hell are we, anyway?"

"GWB," Koda said, pointing up. "Hudson River"— she pointed right—"and we're standing in Fort Washington Point."

Frank glared at me and spat. "Why are we standing under the GWB?"

"Can you pinpoint further?" I asked, ignoring the question. "It's not like Grand Central is the hub of the subway system with thousands of people going through it each day or anything."

"My name is Frank the dragon, not Roger Easton," Frank snapped. "You wanted Street found. I found him."

"Grand Central isn't good enough, dragon," I said, my voice hard. I took a deep breath, exhaling it slowly. "I need his exact location. Find him and bring him to Track 61."

"Who's Roger Easton?" Koda asked. "Is he joining us?"

"Do your homework," I said, and turned to Frank. "Can you get Street or not? Is this beyond your capabilities, mage?"

Frank squared off and blue sparks flew off his body in every direction.

"Are you challenging me?"

"A first-year neophyte can handle this, it's that simple."

"I don't see *you* casting any teleportation circles."

He was playing dirty. Fine.

"As soon as you perfect *your* transmutation casting, I'll start teleporting."

138

"Fuck you, Grey."

"You first, Frank."

"Guys?" Koda asked, concerned.

"So now I'm Frank the ferry?"

"Do *you* want to track down and convince a Transporter to relocate Street?"

"I'll bring him," Frank said with a shake of his tail. "Sucks to be you."

I nodded. "Meet you at 61."

Another arc of electric energy hit the ground, and Frank was gone.

TWENTY-SIX

"What the hell was that?" Koda asked, jumping into the Beast.

I started the engine and let the roar die down to a rumble.

"Sometimes he needs to be reminded he's a mage."

"You two have a strange relationship," Koda replied, attaching her seatbelt gingerly. "You motivate each other with insults?"

"Hey," I said, "thanks for the assist. How banged up are you?"

She waved my words away. "I've had worse. I worked for Hades, remember?"

"True," I acknowledged with a short nod. "Sorry about that. Just that you look how I feel."

"No wonder you make so many friends, your choice of words is astounding."

"It's a gift," I said, reaching into a pocket and pulling out the card Ronin had given me. The sun was creeping over the horizon as I raced downtown before the morning rush. "My friends call me Grey the Friendly."

"What friends?"

"Exactly."

"Grey," Koda started, her voice hitching, and I knew where she was going, "I'm sorry about freezing up back there. It caught me off—"

"You beat it," I said, cutting her off.

"Barely," she said. "I felt it. The walls…"

"We don't have time for a pity party. This isn't the time to start second-guessing yourself. That kind of doubt gets you dead."

"I almost bought it out there," she whispered. "When we face it again—"

"You'll kick its ass…again. That's all I care about. Everyone has fears. Not everyone is willing to face them. You faced yours and overcame them—at least for tonight."

"How come it didn't affect you?"

I knew this question was coming. I could feel her eyes on me. I wanted to say something befitting my station as a Night Warden, something memorable that would bolster her in those dark moments. I thought back to the moment with Darkspirit. It came close this time with its 'observations' about humans.

"I'm one bad day away from an afternoon of the apocalypse," I said, grabbing the thermos and taking a long pull. "There is nothing out there that's scarier than my losing control and laying waste to everything."

"Can you? Have you ever been close?"

"Yes, I can," I said, thinking about the power of Darkspirit. I'd only tapped in to a fraction of its power. "My sword is more powerful than I imagined."

"You ever been close to losing it? I mean besides that time you cratered 6th Avenue?"

"That wasn't my fault. Yes," I said. No sense in sugarcoating shit. It doesn't change the fact that it stinks. "Today, dealing with the rummogres, the sword…tried to make me an offer I couldn't refuse."

"But you said no, right?" Koda asked. "I mean, we wouldn't be having this discussion if you had accepted the offer."

"No, we wouldn't. It was a close—" I started.

"You beat it," she said, cutting me off, using my words. "Like you said, we don't have time for a pity party. Next time it makes you that offer, kick its ass…again."

<I like this warrior. She shows promise.>

"I promise," I said more to myself than to Koda. "If I ever do lose it out there, I'll end it before I hurt anyone."

"Whoa, that's very samurai seppuku of you," she scoffed. "I don't mean to harsh your serious 'superhero sacrificial vibe,' but how about you learn to control the sword instead of the nuclear option?"

"Are you always such a smart-ass?"

"You still have to ask? Seems you aren't paying attention. I have advanced degrees in interpersonal smart-assery. Working on my doctorate in snarkasm."

"I'm sure there's a button around here"—I searched the dashboard—"where I could eject passengers who have overstayed their welcome."

"In your dreams," she said, and I saw the hint of a smile. "You're no Bond, and this isn't an Aston Martin."

"Not even close," I said, patting the dash. "The Beast would snack on an Aston Martin. Can you read that?"

I pointed at the card I gave her. I sped down the Henry Hudson without trying to attract the NYTF. The last thing I needed was Ramirez on my ass for endangering the welfare of the driving public.

143

"Ronin gave this to you?" she asked, looking at both sides.

I knew she'd be able to see the runes and translate them into digits. Her abilities as a cipher encouraged Hades to have her extensively trained in runic languages. With an emphasis on magic and runes, both common and obscure.

"What do those numbers mean to you?"

She focused on the digits. "Either that's one long-ass phone number…wait," she said, pointing. "This top part can be a number, but this part down here, these look like coordinates."

"Coordinates?"

"Don't know where to, but I'm pretty sure. I used to get jobs for Hades like this. No addresses, just coordinates and a target."

"Which part would be the coordinates?" I asked, not familiar with the method. "Just looks like some crazy, international number."

"This part here. Coordinates are always latitude and longitude."

"That much I know."

"These numbers make more sense as latitude and longitude. If we break them up it would read: latitude 40.6994748 and longitude -74.0395587."

"Do you know where that is?"

"Really, old man? Google is your friend."

"I thought with that prodigious brain of yours, you'd be able to just see the number and BOOM—this is the location."

"BOOM—this is the location? Something is seriously damaged with you. Are you sure you didn't hit that tree head first?"

"I'm sure," I answered with an internal shudder. "Barely felt it."

"Head first really makes sense now. Anyway, this was how Hades gave us target sites."

Made sense. Less room for error with coordinates.

"Why would Ronin give me coordinates?"

"Maybe he wants to meet."

I remembered Ronin's words: *"When it looks like you're walking into a trap and you don't know who to trust—use the number."*

I told her what he said.

"You said Aria was a trap," Koda said. "And right now, the amount of people you can trust is down to the fingers on one hand."

"How did he know?"

"Maybe you should give him a call and find out?" she asked. "Ask him why he's trying to get you killed?"

"What I'd like to do is shoot him a few times. He and that book he gave me are the reason the Light Council is out to erase us."

"Technically," she said, raising a finger, "they already wanted to erase you. Or do you mean they want to erase you even more than before?"

"Yes, more than before, and now my apprentice too."

"Do Night Wardens get hazard pay?" she asked. "This job should come with a warning label."

"So should ciphers."

"Warning," she said, extending an arm with a wince, moving it horizontally in front of her, "patrolling the streets of the city with the Night Wardens can result in one or more of the following: premature death, loss of limbs, death, lethal wounds, encounters with creatures that will require years of therapy...for your therapist, death, trauma—both physical and emotional, and lastly—death."

"Sounds about right," I said, turning on 42nd Street and heading across town. It was still early enough to miss the traffic. "Being a warden isn't a job for the weak-willed. You have to be able to face down an enemy knowing you may not walk away, and keep going anyway."

"No," Koda said, shaking her head. "What you just described was Seal Team Six. Night Wardens take that to the next level, the next several levels. Blast past duty and kamikaze right into 'it's our obligation to stop this world-ending monster—we're Night Wardens!' We eat bullets and drink acid…get ready to throw down."

I nodded. "Not too far from the truth."

She stared at me for a few seconds. "And you wonder why there aren't many of you left? Why not give him a call and find out why he set you up…then shoot him."

"I like that plan," I said. "We need a secure line. Even more secure than our comms. He has that sophisticated hi-tech that can probably trace our location."

"I think I know the place. Upper West Side, not far from the park."

"Who lives on the Upper West Side, not far from the park?"

"No one right now," she answered as I made a right at Grand Central and jumped on Park Avenue. "I've only lived here my entire life, but I could swear that building back there is Grand Central Terminal."

"We aren't going to Grand Central."

"But Frank said Street was there," she said, glancing back. "Where are we going?"

"What don't you see? Think, we're starting the morning rush hour. What's missing?"

She looked out the window and took in the scene.

She wasn't a mage, at least not in the conventional sense, but she had heightened abilities and the reflexes to go with them. It didn't take her long.

"Street hasn't been taken over by the Tenebrous."

"How do you know?"

"If he had," she said, still looking around, "this whole area and Grand Central would be in full panic mode. That thing feeds off fear."

"What does that mean, then?"

"Frank found Street and relocated him to this Track 61 you mentioned."

I nodded. "There's hope for you yet, my young apprentice."

"I am not a Sith, ugh."

We parked on the corner of 50th Street, right off Park Avenue, around the corner from the entrance to the Waldorf-Astoria. The Beast was fully outfitted with the proper plates and tags to prevent any sort of towing in the city. More than that, there hadn't been a tow-truck driver brave enough to attempt a tow of the Beast.

I headed over to the pair of brass doors near the corner.

"You feel a need to go to the Waldorf all of a sudden?" Koda asked. "I mean, it's a nice hotel, a little over the top, but still nice."

I pointed at the brass doors on ground level. The sign on one of the doors read "Metro North Emergency Exit 8" and went on to instruct FDNY personnel on what the proper procedure was in case of a fire.

I placed my hand on the left-hand side door, and red runes appeared on the surface. The lock clicked, and the door opened slightly. I was grateful I didn't need to cast, considering I was still recovering from my dance with Fluffy and the rummogres.

147

We headed down a wide corridor where a large freight elevator waited for us. This elevator was created to carry FDR's car when he used to visit. It was easily large enough to fit the Beast inside. I didn't want to take the chance with the runes inside the building and the ones Cecil had put on the Beast. Every so often, runed items could cause magical explosions due to the runes in question having excess volatility.

The Beast was runed with symbols and designs I could barely understand. It felt wise to keep it away from an underground station covered in runes. Even though the Waldorf-Astoria officially denied using Track 61, unofficially, the Dark Council, Hellfire, and other assorted magical groups used the secret entrance for meetings within the lower levels of the hotel.

I wasn't interested in any of that. My only focus was getting to Roosevelt's armored train car. Sitting at the end of Track 61, designated MNCX 002, was the heavily armored and runed train car. I could see the runes giving off a faint blue glow as we approached. Every few seconds, a white flash would erupt from inside the car.

The smell of coffee and honey filled my lungs, with a tinge of chlorine. I heard the low bass of strong magic resonate throughout the station.

"What is that?" Koda asked warily. "That thing looks like a relic."

"It is," I said while I admired it. "When those doors are closed, that train car is nearly impossible to breach. You'd need the equivalent of a runic nuclear blast to make a dent in those runes."

"Is that where…?"

"Yes, he's in there," Frank said from behind us. "Did you bring the exit strategy?"

"I'm going to get one now."

"Enjoy that trip down memory lane," Frank said. "Lockpick, you'd better let him go solo on this one. Transporters are a twitchy bunch, but they like him for some reason. Also, the price of admission is steep. Grey is a masochist, I think."

Koda looked at me. "You going to be okay down here, old man?" she asked. "You didn't bring your glasses, so you may end up lost, wandering around the tracks. Would hate to have to mount a search-and-rescue for your old ass."

"I don't wear glasses."

"That's called denial. Lack of use does not imply you don't need them."

"I'll be fine," I said, heading back down the tracks, away from the armored car. "If I'm not back in twenty—get inside and seal the doors."

"No way," Frank answered and spat, flicking his tail nervously. "Get your ass back here in ten. Rummers were all over Street. We lost them, but they'll find him again."

"What happens if we seal the car?" Koda asked.

"If that car is sealed," Frank said as I walked away, "it's so damn old, it'll take an Arch Mage to open it again. They had names for these kinds of spaces during the war."

"What did they call them?" Koda asked, her voice getting fainter with each step.

"Tombs."

TWENTY-SEVEN

As powerful as Frank was, there was no way he was going to breach the Cloister's defenses. Neither was Fluffy, for that matter. In order to get Street to Aria in one piece, I needed a Transporter.

Transporters were magic-users with one specific ability: they were master teleporters. No mage could match a transporter's speed, level of precision, or power.

<What are you looking for, mage?>

"Not what, who," I said. "And I'm not speaking to you."

<Not speaking to me? Ludicrous, we are bonded—one. I know your thoughts.>

"You tried to go psychosword on me," I said. "What the hell?"

<I was merely pointing out your options. Did we not dispatch the creatures with ease? That was a fraction of my power. Imagine what you could do with all my power.>

"That's exactly what I don't want to imagine."

<You fear me? No, it's not fear. What is this sensation? >

"I'm humbled by the power you contain," I said.

"Unleashing all of you? I don't trust anyone with that much power, starting with myself."

<Humbled? The power is yours to claim, mage. To exert dominion over those who would threaten you—threaten us.>

"Wait a minute…are you scared?"

<Preposterous. I am a goddess.>

"In the body of a sword. What happens if the sword is destroyed, I wonder?"

<You would die. Suddenly and painfully, I might add.>

"That, I know. What I want to know is, what would happen to you?"

<If our bond were severed, your death would be immediate, and I...I would...I would find another bondmate.>

"But you can't do that on your own," I said, letting my senses expand throughout the tracks. "Hades had to give you to me this time."

<I'd prefer not to discuss the matter at this time.>

"Oh, so now you're not talking to me? What happened to 'ludicrous, we are bonded—one'?"

Silence.

"Well, at least I know how to get you to be silent for a while."

I wasn't in any condition to cast after my skirmish with Fluffy. I was counting on my energy signature being the bait for the nearest Transporter. If I broke out the truffles, they would rush me and take the chocolate and then vanish. Transporters did not play when it came to chocolate.

I wasn't looking forward to this. In order for a Transporter to interact with you, they needed to 'know' you. No, not in the Biblical sense. This went beyond the physical.

Transporters needed to 'read' your runic signature before they would shift you to where you wanted to go. Your deepest emotions would be exposed and raw. It was about as pleasant as it sounded. I was never a fan of raw, exposed emotions, but if I didn't get Street out of here, Fluffy would take over his body and kill him—or worse, use him to kill others, which meant I would have to ghost Street.

I let my senses expand and felt out the station. My range was much shorter underground, at most eighty meters or so, if I pushed it. I jumped down off one of the platforms and walked farther onto the tracks.

Every station usually had one Transporter, you just had to know where to find them. Sometimes they lurked on the platforms, but most often they stayed on the tracks between stations.

A hub like Penn or Grand Central had about a dozen Transporters strategically situated throughout the station to handle the flow of teleportation. Because Track 61 wasn't officially a part of the subway, I had to walk some distance before the subtly sweet sensation hit me. I felt her energy signature between stations, approaching slowly. I let my energy flow even stronger, giving her plenty of notice as to my presence. They didn't like to be startled.

TWENTY-EIGHT

I saw her sitting on some abandoned stairs that led nowhere. She sat hunkered down as if battling a bitter frost. She looked up at the sound of my footsteps. I deliberately made some noise on my approach. Not that it mattered. You couldn't really sneak up on a Transporter.

She smiled and narrowed her eyes when she saw me, waving me closer. I could never tell them apart. Every Transporter looked the same.

Once, while studying the phenomena of Transporters in a Quantum Runic class, a junior professor Ziller once posited the theory that there was only one Transporter, existing at different points in time, simultaneously encountering all the different versions of 'you' across your timeline. I'd failed that class.

That junior professor went on to chair the department, melting young mage brains with regularity for years afterward. I could argue that it was his book that had set off the chain of events I currently found myself in. I was sure he would argue otherwise and proceed to undo what little hold I had on reality.

The Transporter appeared to be an old woman wrapped in too many layers. It was the perfect camouflage in the city. I was never able to determine what race they belonged to. I just knew they weren't human. I don't know how she wasn't melting down here in this infernal heat. If it wasn't because the duster had saved my ass more times than I could count, I would have left it with Frank and Koda.

Sweat formed on my brow. Wiping it away was as effective as trying to mop up the ocean. It was just too hot down here. I stepped close and crouched down.

"Hello, grandmother," I said as she placed a hand on my cheek. It was cool to the touch and I felt my sweat evaporate. Suddenly it wasn't so hot. "I need a shift."

"Do you now?" she asked, her voice resonating throughout the space.

"It's not for me," I said. "I have a friend in danger, and I need him moved somewhere safe, somewhere far from here that's protected."

"There is no place closed to me." She outstretched a hand. I sighed, bracing myself for the inevitable chastising, placing my hand in hers. She shook her head, tutting at me. "You've stepped over to the dark side, boy, haven't you?"

My first thought was I stepped into the dark the day I'd ended Jade's life. That's when it started.

"Yes, I stepped over," I said. "If it means I can stop someone else from taking my path, then yes, I embrace the dark."

She shook her head again and looked up at me.

"You need to let her go, my child," she said. "She's gone. Nothing you can do will return her to you. No good will come of holding her in your heart like this."

"No," I said, my voice hard. I pulled my hand

gently out of hers. "In my heart is the only place I can see her as she was. I need her to stay there a little longer, at least until I'm done."

Arguing with a Transporter was probably not the wisest course of action. Especially when it was documented that they were immensely powerful beings of unknown origin.

It just so happened that every time I saw a Transporter, they triggered my Jade memories. It felt almost intentional—a thought I kept to myself. I was bold, but not *that* bold. The bass notes around the Transporter let me know I was dealing with 'out of my league' power. Even with Darkspirit, this 'old woman' could probably blink me out of this plane with a thought. Not a theory I felt like testing.

She wagged her finger at me and narrowed her eyes.

"If you keep this darkness too close to your heart, it will spread to everything you touch, everyone you know," she said. "You need to let it go."

I wasn't sure if she was referring to my memory of Jade, the darkness, or Darkspirit. The last thing I was about to do was ask her to explain what she meant. That wasn't how these things ever worked. I was left to figure out the meaning on my own—it was part of the design.

"Can you help me, grandmother?" I asked. "It's important."

"Where does your friend need to go?"

"I need him safe." I probably should've given Aria a heads-up about the incoming unstable mage. I'd let her kill me later. "Please send him to Aria at the Wordweavers."

The Transporter closed her eyes. I didn't know if she was tired, taking a nap, or triangulating angles of deflection. After a few seconds, she nodded.

"Do you have something for me?" she asked expectantly.

I reached in my pocket and pulled out four boxes of La Madeline au Truffle from Knipschildt. Transporters didn't accept money as payment. A trinket of some kind could work if you needed a short shift. For something like this, I needed the heavy hitters.

"Will this do?" I asked. "It's all I have."

It was always best to play the humble card with Transporters. I'd heard stories about them refusing to interact if you made it seem like what you were giving them was off the charts. Granted, La Madeline au Truffle clocked in at $250 a box, but this was Street. A grand in chocolate to keep him safe was a price I was willing to pay.

I extended the boxes to her. She took a moment to open and smell the truffles and an enormous smile crossed her lips. The smell of chocolate and cinnamon filled the air. The next second, the boxes were gone. I don't know where or how, but being masters of teleportation, I assumed moving chocolate was simplicity itself.

The smile remained on her face as she shuffled over, away from the stairs.

"Yes, that will be adequate," she said. "Your friend is the mage in the train car. His name is Street, is it not?"

"Yes," I said, not surprised she knew this information. "That's him."

"He seems a bit unstable." She gestured. "That should calm him."

"He's had a rough life," I said. "I promised I would look after him."

"Despite the darkness in and around you, Grey Stryder, you still possess much light."

I wasn't about to argue that my heart was as black as they came. If she saw light in the nooks and crannies, I'd take it.

She spread her hands apart, and a large runic circle formed under my feet. It transitioned from red to green to blue in a loop of bright colors.

"What are you doing?" I said, looking down at the circle. "The shift is for him, not me."

"I know," she said, still smiling. "You are going home, to repay your generosity."

"Home?" I asked, suddenly confused. "What home?"

"You have more than one?"

She must've meant The Dive—which was currently occupied with the Light Council. The same Light Council that wanted me dead. This was going to be bad.

"Are you prepared?" she asked. "Your friend will go to the Wordweavers, the mage-lizard and the phantom girl will go home with you."

"Prepared? No. Prepared for what? What are you talking about? I can't go home. There are people there waiting to inflict maximum damage."

"Not anymore," she said. "Now, listen closely, Warden. This teleport requires you to listen to my instructions and not deviate. Do you understand?"

"No?"

"Good," she said with a chuckle. "Now, take a jump to the left!"

I complied, jumping over to the left. I looked at the ground, thinking I had to dodge something.

"Very good, Warden." The air around her began to take on a golden hue. "Now, a step to the right."

I stepped to the right but noticed there was nothing on the ground beneath me.

"Excellent, the cast is going well," she said,

chuckling even more. "A few more steps. Please place both hands on your hips."

"Both hands on my what?"

"Did I stutter, young man?"

"No, grandmother," I said, placing both hands on my hips. "This is ridiculous."

"Oh, are you the Transporter all of a sudden? Do you know how to execute a mass teleport of allies and enemies from a location? Sight unseen, without killing anyone?"

"No, ma'am," I said under my breath. The light around her grew brighter still.

"Correct, you can't," she said, shuffling around behind me. "Now, bring your knees in tight."

"My what?"

"Knees, in tight," she said, adjusting my legs and pushing my lower back, forcing my pelvis forward. "Don't forget the pelvic thrust."

"You've got to be kidding me."

"Yes, I am, Night Warden," she said. "Stop taking yourself so seriously."

At this point she was cackling, and I was certain I looked entirely foolish. That's when I knew. Transporters were just old ladies who had lost their minds. Wonderful.

"I don't understand this at all," I said, pulling on my duster and straightening out.

"I know," she said with a nod. "It will be clear—or it won't be."

The glow surrounding her was too bright to look at directly.

A transporter shift violated most of Ziller's known laws of time and space. Rather than teleporting you where you wanted to go, it warped time, space, and gravity around you so that the place you wanted to go aligned to your location. The one time that Professor Ziller had put this on a test, several mages had to be carried out of the classroom. Apparently, their brains had seized.

When you were aligned, the Transporter would give you the equivalent of a runic kick and send you down the bridge she created. No mage in history had been able to teleport using this method. In all my studies, I'd never read or heard where it required such strange body motions.

"What does that even mean?"

"Exactly," she said. "I will speak to you soon, Night Warden. Thank you for the exquisite chocolate. I hope my gift was worthy of yours."

I closed my eyes against the light and felt the world tilt sideways.

TWENTY-NINE

W hen I opened my eyes, I stared into the face of a thorny dragon.

"If you spit on me, I'm going to shoot you."

The familiar smell of honey, coffee, and cinnamon filled my lungs.

"He's alive," Frank said, moving off my chest. "Told you it would take more than that to kill him. He's like a roach…indestructible."

"Don't sound so excited," I said, sitting up slowly as the floor stopped its tilting. "Where are we?"

"The Dive, I think," Koda said, looking around. "How did we get here? We were just at Track 61."

"Track 61," I said. "Street."

"Aria just called," Cole said. "He's there in stasis and in a null unit. At least until you deal with whatever is after him."

I breathed out a sigh of relief. I noticed The Dive was empty. This in and of itself wasn't odd. I checked the time. It was still morning.

"How long have I been gone?" I asked. "When was the last time you saw me?"

Cole gave me a look, shook his head, and started pouring coffee.

"Two years ago, to the day. You and Koda disappeared. We'd lost hope, but now...now you're back and you can set things right."

"You know I can see the calendar behind you, right?"

"Shit, I knew I forgot something. What's wrong with you? You left here last night. Do I need to get your bed at Haven prepped?"

"I don't have a bed at Haven."

"You should," Cole said, heading to the back room. "Whatever or whoever dropped you guys off, removed everyone from The Dive except me. We are going to have some pissed-off customers later."

"And an even more pissed-off Light Council, "I said with a small smile. "Serves them right."

I thought back to the Transporter and started laughing. She was right, of course. Damn Time Warp. Don't know how I missed it.

Koda looked at Frank.

"Does he usually do this?" Koda asked nervously. "I've never seen him laugh before. Is he going to hurt himself?"

"Laugh?" Frank asked as he stepped close. "He laughs all the time."

"Really?" Koda asked, stepping away from me. "All the time?"

"In fact, back in the day, they used to call him Grey, the Jolly Night Warden," Frank scoffed. "Of course not. It's clear he's suffered some kind of psychotic break. A little shock therapy should straighten him right out."

My hand was a blur as I drew Fatebringer and brought the muzzle to Frank's head.

"If I feel so much as a twinge of static electricity heading my way, there's going to be a lizard motif all over the wall."

"Look at that," Frank said, stepping back slowly. "Instant cure. Damn, I'm good."

I got to my feet and made my way to the bar...and the coffee.

"Beast?" I growled.

"Outside," Cole said, "scaring neighbors as usual. If you can get whoever delivered you to handle some of the inventory shipments, I'd pay extra for that service."

I took a long sip of coffee.

"Koda," I said, waving her over, "Upper West Side. Elaborate."

"It's a pretty high-end address. One of Hades' places."

"Hades owns half the city. Be a little more specific."

"His wife, Persephone, keeps a place uptown, which is why we had an observation post nearby."

"He spies on his wife?"

"Spies? No. We were the security detail. She knew we were there and invited us over all the time," Koda answered. "She's not a helpless waif, you know. She's a goddess."

"I'm kind of over goddesses right about now," I said, thinking about Izanami.

"She just wanted her own space. She liked her alone-time, so she and Hades compromised. She could be alone as long as we were close."

"So, you're telling me you...what, camped outside?"

She glared at me. "You sure you weren't teleported minus the brain? We stayed in the tower adjacent to hers, in another apartment. We were literally five seconds away with the portal system Hades set up.

"Where was this, again?"

"The Eldorado."

"That's where we're going to make the call to Ronin," I said. "Get ready. Can you still get into this apartment?"

"I can get into any apartment," she said smugly. "Hasn't been a door built that can stop me."

"Not if it's in the Central Archive," I said, heading up the stairs. "Their security seems to be cipher-proof."

Her face darkened, and Frank chuckled.

"Ouch," Frank said from the bar. "Burned by the ancient Night Warden. I guess some ciphers must operate under a limited warranty."

Frank disappeared a second later with a crack of lightning. A fan nearly sliced him in half.

"Keep it up, lizard," Koda said as the fan returned to her hand. "I'm going to cut you down to size."

"Her aim is shit too," Frank yelled upstairs. "I think this cipher is defective. Can we return her, Grey?"

"I'll give you defective," Koda yelled, followed by glass breaking.

I closed the door to my room and took a breath. I was going to have to call another mage, and this call needed to be private. I activated all the runes and fail-safes. These were actually Koda-proof and would stop her with a nasty jolt if she tried to get past them and into my room.

I sat in my circle and centered my breathing. The Tenebrous was still out there somewhere. Even though Street was safe, other mages were still in danger. Redrum X was still flooding the streets, and I wasn't any closer to the supplier. I couldn't make a move against the Redrum X distribution until I dealt with Fluffy.

I didn't know the status of the Cloisters, but I had

to operate under the premise that they were compromised somehow. So, I had to make the call. There were two reasons for this. One was to get more information on the soulblaze, and the other was to facilitate getting a warden bag. This mage wasn't dark, but he didn't exactly follow rules.

I pressed my comm. "Dexter," I said, "global acquisition."

The comm would reach out anywhere on the planet, boosted by the circle I sat in. If Dexter was on this plane, it would locate him. After a few seconds, a voice spoke into my ear.

"Aye, this had better be good or you'll have an angry Morrigan to deal with."

"Hello, Dex," I said with a sigh. "Please extend my apologies to the Morrigan."

"Grey! It's been a dog's age," he yelled. "What cataclysm are you ass deep in this time?"

"I need a soulblaze to destroy a Tenebrous."

"Oh, shite," he said. "I'll be right over."

THIRTY

Poindexter Montague was a fearsome mage of questionable repute.

He wasn't exactly a dark mage, more like a gray mage. His semi-tarnished reputation was attributed mostly to whom he chose as a partner. Something I could now strangely identify with.

Dex was currently involved in a serious relationship with the Morrigan. She was the Celtic goddess of Death and War. This wasn't a symbiotic situation like Izanami and me. He really cared for her and, it seemed—surprisingly, she had actual feelings for him. I didn't know how it worked, just that it did. Honestly, I didn't want the details, but I was certain Dex would share anyway.

I felt the pressure of the room shift and smelled fresh-cut grass as a green circle formed in the center of the room. The high-pitched sound of a wind chime tinkled throughout my room as a portal formed, and Dex stepped in. Usually, when I was in the presence of serious magical power, I'd hear the foghorn of doom. Wind chimes meant I was in the presence of power several magnitudes greater.

At least this time he was dressed. Well, at least

169

partially dressed. He wore a kilt and not much else. His gray hair was disheveled and longer than usual, and he was traveling *sans* raven.

"Hope you don't mind the attire," he said, looking around with a chuckle. "Sounded like a bit of an emergency. You have anything to eat? I'm feeling a bit peckish. That woman, I swear, she's going to wear me down to a nub if she keeps this up."

I took in the sight and smiled despite myself.

"Maybe you ought to slow down a bit, pace yourself?"

"She's a goddess, lad," Dex said, looking around again. "There's no slowing down with her. Where's the lizard?"

"Frank?"

"Yes, I owe him a right blast of energy for his last prank," he said with a chuckle. "Devious little dragon. Wait until I see him. He's going to be tickled pink."

I didn't know what the prank was, and I didn't want to know. A prank for Frank could be as simple as electrifying some mage's house, or as complicated as having the same mage hit by a bolt of lightning when he opened the door to his home. What I did know was that it wasn't happening in The Dive.

A few, meaning the more powerful ones, thought Frank was funny in a twisted way. Most everyone else wanted to shred him and, by default, me, for some reason. And people wondered why I had no friends.

"Frank is downstairs being his usual. I need your help now."

"I'll leave a special thank you for him at the bar downstairs," Dex said with an evil grin. "Please make sure he gets it. You're going to need this."

He handed me a small card with a short set of runes.

"Will it explode The Dive?"

"Absolutely not," Dex said.

"Will it explode Frank?"

"I can honestly say it will not explode your bar or the lizard, but it will make your dragon fuchsia for a week. Unless you cast that reversal spell."

"Only for a week?" I asked. "He's going to be pissed… I love it."

Dex laughed. "He's naturally paranoid, so you're going to have to sell it."

"I can sell it, trust me," I said. "You don't have a shirt? Really?"

"Ach, my manly physique intimidates you. I understand," Dex said, flexing his pecs. "The Morrigan loves me topless. I have to say…I return the sentiment."

"No, you don't have to say, but thanks."

I tossed him one of my shirts to cover the runes.

His upper body was a mosaic of scars, or at least it looked that way from a distance. Unlike my photo-reactive ink runes, which appeared invisible until hit with certain light, and under the right conditions, Dex had runes etched directly into his skin in a process closely resembling scarification.

That, plus his immense magical knowledge in several disciplines, made him a dangerous adversary and a powerful ally. You don't get to be over a thousand years old as a mage by being mediocre.

Two lines of text surrounded by more runes were tattooed on each of his forearms. My Latin was rusty, but I still remembered enough to decipher his ink. One read *dum spiro spero*, 'While I breathe, I hope.' On the other it read *deponite omnes spes*, 'Abandon all hope.' Those two lines pretty much summed up Dex. He gave you hope when things seemed hopeless.

"I'll have Cole bring up some food."

"No need," he said with a sly grin. "I just ate."

"Really?" I asked, shaking my head. "Does the Morrigan know you speak like this?"

"Know? She's worse than I am."

"You're hopeless."

"What? I was referring to my heavy meal of sausage and beans, which she, of course, shared with me," he said with another grin. "You really need to get your mind out of the gutter, boy."

"I do? Really?"

He narrowed his eyes at me and grew serious.

"How long have you had the dark blade?" he asked, sitting on my trunk, spreading his legs, and burning the worst possible image of his junk into my retinas. "Oh, and you're bonded too?"

"It's a long story," I said, averting my eyes. "Can you do something about the clothes?"

"My lady loves me like this—easy access, don't you know?"

"I do know, thanks," I said. "How about we try some pants...even shorts would work."

He looked down. "Since when did Night Wardens become such prudes?"

"I'm not a prude," I said. "It's good to see you, I just didn't expect to see so *much* of you."

"If I told you some of the stories when I went out on patrols with the Wardens...tch, those were some good times," he said wistfully. "But we aren't here to discuss my misspent youth."

Dex was one of the reasons, if not *the* reason, patrols banned outside assistance and were limited only to Night Wardens. Several of his *patrols* involved plenty of alcohol, succubi, and all-night lovefests.

"I'm sure they were great times."

His dark eyes focused on me. "How bad is it?"

"Mages are dying in the streets."

"Dark Council?"

"Can't be bothered, plus the vamp is missing, so they're dealing with factional in-fighting."

"Mages, weres, and vamps? Bad idea from the start...NYTF?"

"This is above all their paygrades. Ramirez can't keep up."

"Did you contact my nephew and his partner? They're a little on the explosive side, but excellent in a pinch. He's a Montague, after all."

"Your nephew and I have worked cases together. I think a Tenebrous would be too dangerous at his age," I said. "Plus, I'd like to keep the buildings standing, and they have a habit of remodeling them into rubble."

"Too true," Dex said, nodding his head. "Dare I say it...Light Council?"

"Presently trying to kill me on suspicion of trying to blow up the Central Archive and trying to kill Honor."

"Again?" Dex smiled, stood up, and clapped me on the back. "Gotta stay with the classics. They always were a group of stuffed shirts. What really happened?"

I explained about Ronin, the book and the events that led to the Light Council wanting both Koda's and my head on a platter.

"You can't trust Division 13," Dex said somberly with a shake of his head. "I have some contacts there but, like I said, you can't trust them. There's always some hidden agenda, they can't help themselves. Do you want me to call in the Ten?"

"You don't think that's overkill?"

"Aye," Dex said. "If you get them involved, it'd better be some end-of-the-world event. They'll be bored otherwise."

"I do need you to speak to LD and TK for me, though."

"Oh? That pair is usually enough for most cataclysms."

"No, I need a warden bag."

"Warden bag? Haven't seen one of those in centuries, but if they're still out there, Fordey would be the place. I'll send word. If it's a bag, you need to see TK."

"Can't I just speak to LD?"

"Aye, I understand your reluctance," Dex said with a nod. "Between us, she's not as bad as the rumors."

"Really? Because the rumors are pretty bad."

"Aye, she's much worse than the rumors," he said with a wide smile. "But if you're looking for a bag, she's the one to see."

"Fantastic," I said. "That won't suck at all."

"It's not so bad," Dex said. "If you don't piss her off, and pay the cost, you'll get your bag. If not, well, you're dying anyway, and she'll just speed up the process. In any case, that's not the immediate concern.

"Glad to hear my imminent demise is not high on the to-do list."

"You're a Night Warden, imminent demise is called stepping out of the door for the evening's patrol," Dex said, waving my words away. "Do you know who summoned the Tenebrous?"

"I don't know," I said. "Been dealing with rummers and these new rummogres."

"Rummogres?"

"Hybrid creatures. Rummer and ogres combined into one convenient monstrous package," I explained. "They're fast, intelligent, and hit like a truck."

"How many of these rummogre things have you seen?

"Three so far," I said. "Are you saying I should expect more?"

"Has the Tenebrous found a host?"

"Not yet," I said. "He threatened a friend, whom I had relocated to safety."

"It," Dex said. "Not 'he.' These things aren't human."

"No, they aren't," I said, thinking about the bloody and dying mage. "It wears humans like garments."

"They don't just appear," Dex said, shaking his head. "They are creatures formed of hate and fear. Have you angered anyone, or made any enemies lately?"

I stared at him, and he stared back. Both of us remained silent for a good three seconds before he burst out in laughter.

"Are you serious?" I said with a tight smile. "The question is: who haven't I pissed off?"

"Oh, so your face *can* make a smile, good. There's still hope for you, then."

"I need to learn this soulblaze, Dex. It's the only thing that will work against it."

"Wrong," Dex said. "You're old enough to know better. Usually when someone says this is the 'only way,' something can be done, it just means—?"

"They lack creativity," I said, answering the obvious. "The soulblaze is the most effective way?"

"Not particularly," Dex answered. "The most effective way would be to remove the summoner, since he or she is the anchor for the Tenebrous. Since you don't know who that is, I'll have to show you the soulblaze."

"You know it?"

"Did you call me here for my good looks?"

"Not particularly, no."

"Ach, you cut me to the quick, boy."

"I thought you wanted an honest answer."

"Where vanity is concerned, honesty is overrated. Remember that, and you'll live a longer life."

"Duly noted. You can show me the soulblaze?"

"Yes, we only have one minor problem."

"Problem? Is the rune too difficult?"

"The problem isn't with the rune. The problem is with you."

"With me?"

Dex nodded. "You've bonded with a dark blade. If you cast the soulblaze, it will be the last thing you cast, ever. That spell will kill you."

THIRTY-ONE

"Kill me?"

"Do you still want me to teach it to you?"

"Yes."

"Are you sure you don't want to call my nephew? Tristan can be a bit particular, but he's an excellent mage. Still a little green, but good in a tight spot, and you, my boy, are in one of the tightest. Reminds me of this succubus—"

"Does he have any fears?" I interrupted.

"Hmm, there is that," Dex said, tapping his chin. "When he was young, he feared getting his uniform wrinkled or soiled. That, and cold tea. He *was* a peculiar child. I told Nana to stop coddling him."

"I see. He hasn't changed much, then."

"That...is a fear of a loss of control," Dex answered, his voice hard. "Most mages possess this fear. Except, maybe you. Or you've buried it so deep, you can't recognize it anymore."

"Tristan can't help me with this," I said. "Neither can Simon with his devil-dog. They care about each other too much. The Tenebrous would use that fear of loss against them, paralyze them, and then either end them, or take them."

"You speak the truth," Dex answered after a pause. "You don't have those attachments, do you? Friends, your associates"—he looked around—"this place?"

"I can't *afford* those attachments, Dex," I said, keeping my voice cold. "The cost...the price...is too high. And I've already paid it once. I'm not paying it again."

"Without those attachments, you don't have a life. All you're doing is existing."

"Yet, I'm the only one who can face this thing."

"Only one?" Dex asked. "No, not the *only one*."

"The most effective one, then," I said. "I'll pay the cost, so no one else has to."

Dex shook his head. We'd had this conversation in the past. He wanted me to open up and let people in; I wanted to retreat further into my grief and solitude. We always ended up in the same place, with me being alone.

"You can't do everything alone, boy. That way madness lies."

"In a mad world, only the mad are sane," I answered. "Let me do what I need to do...what I *can* do."

Dex sighed and nodded.

"If you cast this, it will act the opposite of a siphon," Dex said, showing me the gestures and symbols. "Your blade is the counterpart to Simon's. I'm assuming it acts as a siphon, yes?"

"Yes," I said, remembering the darkness after I cut Fluffy's latest victim. "It requires blood."

"Those blades usually do," Dex said. "The soulblaze will weaponize yours, and the blade's energy signature, allowing you to wield it as a blast. It's called a soulblaze because it's an illuminated energy signature spell. This light...the light of your

178

essence, is what will do damage to the Tenebrous. This is a one-time-use spell. Do you understand?"

"What happens after I use it?"

"If you miss—you're too drained to do anything else but lay there and die."

"And if I don't miss?"

"You'll destroy the Tenebrous, and then you'll be devoid of any energy signature or essence. You'll be a shell, too drained to do anything but to be still for a few minutes, and then you'll die."

"I'm sensing a theme with this spell."

"It's a battle spell, designed for use against enemy combatants during times of war. Mages would cast it on captured prisoners and use their soulblazes against their own people. It was lethal and efficient, killing enemy and prisoner in one fell swoop."

"How long?"

Dex flexed his jaw and stared in my eyes.

"Ten seconds."

"Ten seconds until I expire, or ten seconds of soulblaze?"

"Once you activate this spell, it's locked, it will fire for ten seconds. No more, no less. You can direct the blast through a focus of your choosing. I'd suggest your sword, since you will be merging energies anyway."

"Can it be interrupted?"

"Of course, by killing the mage before he unleashes it."

"That kind of interrupts everything."

"Don't be in a hurry to rush into the secret house of death."

"Life is a walking shadow and this time I'm the poor player."

"At least you kept up with your readings," Dex said.

179

"Like I had a choice."

"Once the spell runs its course…so does the mage. I think you should reconsider. Find the summoner and stop them."

"Don't have that kind of time, Dex. Thank you. If I don't see you again…"

He nodded. "Understood. I'll make sure the ceremony is a proper Warden ceremony, if it comes to that."

"Can't ask for more than that," I said. "I appreciate the assist."

"Ach, can't help but think I just helped you kill yourself."

"How can you kill someone who's already dead?"

"Indeed," Dex said and paused. "Remember, the ones who stand with you when it's all gone to shite aren't there for the sights and attractions. That's your family."

"I don't have—"

"Don't interrupt me when I'm speaking, boy."

I remained silent. It was always best to stay on the good side of a mage like Dex.

"You lost someone. Hell, we've all lost someone," he said, pointing a finger. "Hold them in your heart if you must, but don't neglect the ones standing next to you, shedding blood on the field, or one day you'll find yourself on that same field shedding blood alone. Ye understand?"

I nodded in reply. "I understand."

"Good. You honor those who risk their lives with you, or else what good are you?"

Dex formed a portal, gave me a short nod, and disappeared, leaving me alone.

THIRTY-TWO

"What the hell was that?" Frank asked when I reached the ground floor. "Who did you have up there?"

"Dex," I said, keeping my voice serious, expecting the reaction. "He says hello."

"Did you say Dex?" Frank asked, flicking his tail rapidly "And you didn't call me?"

"It wasn't a social visit," I said. "In case you haven't noticed, we nearly got our asses ghosted last night. No one has time for pranks right now."

"I just wanted to say hello," Frank answered quietly. "He does happen to be a friend."

"A friend?" I asked angrily. "What the hell are *you* doing? Some of us are trying to save lives, while you want to do…what? Have a beer with friends?"

"Shit," Frank replied. "No need to get your panties in a bunch. I was at the bridge last night too, remember?"

I glared at Koda in silence until she saw my expression. "We have a call to make. You coming?"

She looked at Cole. "Did you make his coffee strong?"

"Apparently not strong *enough*," Cole said. "Want some to go?"

"What I *want*," I started, "is for my apprentice to be ready to go when it's time to leave, and for my supposed head-of-security lizard to lock down the place, so it doesn't get camped out in by the Light Council again. That's what I want."

"Fuck you, Grey," Frank said, moving to the end of the bar. "What's this?"

Cole shrugged. "No clue. Some old guy left it here for you. Said he knew you."

"Maybe the head of security should, oh, I don't know, secure the area?"

Frank gave me a one-finger salute as he approached the package.

"Cole, we seem to be low on some of the Glenfiddich," I said, adding an edge to my voice. "Would it be too much to ask to keep the bar properly stocked?"

Cole raised an eyebrow. "Excuse me? I always keep the bar—"

"Now would be a good time," I said, standing at the door with Koda behind me.

"Better listen to the Warden Emperor, Cole," Frank said. "He's liable to shoot you today, just to get his point across."

"If that's what it takes to get things done around here," I said, letting my hand rest on Fatebringer, "I can shoot to wound."

Cole left the bar and headed downstairs, giving me a one-finger salute goodbye.

"You know you don't have to be such a dick," Frank started. "Just because you're having a rough—"

"*You* don't tell me what I need to do, lizard," I said, pointing at the package and opening the door. "I tell *you* what to do. You're the head of security—do some securing."

I stepped outside, closed the door, reactivated the defensive runes...and waited. Koda stood next to me, beside herself with barely controlled anger.

"What the hell? Bite my head off, Mr. Night Warden."

I raised a finger. "Wait for it," I whispered.

I heard Frank cursing, and I put my ear to the door.

"*Secure* my ass. Just wait until the next time he calls, needing me."

There was a ripping of paper and then I heard the small *thwump*, followed by much louder cursing.

"Goddammit, Grey! Grey!" Frank yelled. "I know you're out there, you bastard!"

I deactivated the runes and opened the door a crack. Koda peeked in behind me and burst into laughter.

"Holy hell," I heard Cole say. "That is so not your color...Pinky."

Not only was Frank hot-pink, he was a glowing hot-pink. I slid the card Dex gave me me through the crack and whispered a small spell so it would land on the far end of the bar, next to Cole. I saw him pick it up and look at me with a nod and a small smile.

"I know you're out there, Grey," Frank yelled again, as I closed the door and activated the defensive runes. "This was that bastard, Dex, and you knew, Grey. You're supposed to be a friend! Don't worry, I'm a patient dragon. I will have my vengeance!"

"Holy shit, that is pink," Koda said around another giggle. "That was all a setup?"

"I can sell it when I need to," I said, enjoying the moment of levity. "Let's go make that call."

"Where's my bike?" Koda asked, looking around. "They said they delivered it."

"They did. I had SuNaTran pick it up."

"I told you, I don't know how they saw me, but it wasn't—"

"Cecil picked it up to enhance the camouflage," I said, raising a hand when I sensed she was going to jump into a rant about her abilities. "It's to incorporate what you encountered at the Central Archive. Seems Rahbi informed him of your 'difficulty' remaining unseen, and he's working to rectify the situation—at least for the Shroud."

"I will get in there," Koda said, determined. "And they won't have a clue."

"Do me a favor," I said. "Can it wait until they aren't trying to kill us on sight and after we've dealt with our current situation?"

"Fine," she said, getting into the Beast. "Let's go."

"I've only been saying that for an hour."

I jumped into the Beast, started the roaring engine and sped off to The Eldorado.

THIRTY-THREE

"What do we know so far?" I asked as we raced uptown.

"Apparently, you have a sense of humor," Koda said, suppressing a smile. "Who knew?"

"No one," I said. "And it will be denied if it's ever brought up in public. Now, focus."

"Street is at the Cloisters."

"Confirmed, in stasis and in a null room," I said. "Fluffy will have a hard time getting to him. Too many layers of security. Which means?"

"Street is now a hard target."

"And that means?"

"Fluffy will go after softer targets: more mages on the streets or in the park."

"We don't want that," I said, with a nod. "What else?"

"We still have the Redrum X problem. Don't know who's the supplier or how it's being distributed."

"Correct. What's the priority?"

She remained silent for a few seconds, as she thought this one through. If we went after the Redrum, we've still left Fluffy loose to prey on the defenseless. If we went after Fluffy, Redrum X would still be unleashed on the streets.

Fluffy was the immediate threat.

"We need to use our resources," she said after more thought. "How much heat can you take from the Light Council?"

"My duster can withstand a dragon blast—a *real* dragon blast."

"I'm guessing Ronin is using us as a proxy, to do what he can't or won't do, so he can remain behind the scenes. While you were upstairs, I ran the coordinates he gave you."

"Where do they lead?"

"Ellis Island," she said. "It's possible the person who summoned Fluffy is on that island, or someone connected to the Redrum is there. Either way, Ronin wants you to check it out."

"Or, it's a trap, and we walk into a Light Council welcoming party of pain."

"What's the play?" she asked. "We can't just let him use us."

"We let the Light Council know we're going to the island. They storm it, and deal with whatever they find there."

"Right. You can summon Fluffy," she said. "Let's pick somewhere better this time."

"Even though that means another duster," I said. "Aria is going to kill me."

"We arrange a battleground on our terms, not his, and end his ass. That's the only part I'm getting stuck on."

"What?"

"Will your sword work on the Tenebrous? I don't think my fans can inflict damage on that level."

"I'll deal with Fluffy," I said, as we pulled up to the

side of The Eldorado on 91st Street. "Let's go use our resources."

The entrance to the building on 91st was unmanned, used by service personnel only. It bypassed the front desk and led directly to the elevators. Koda walked past the main elevators and lobby, turning the corner to a narrow hallway. At the end of the hallway was another, smaller, elevator door.

"This leads straight to the North Tower," she said, pressing the wall next to the elevator. "Direct access."

The wall gave off a faint orange glow, and the elevator call button lit up. The elevator arrived a few seconds later. We stepped in, and Koda pressed another panel inside, closing the doors. I noticed the redundancy in fail-safes.

"It reads runic signatures?"

She nodded. "Yes, it's the only way it will work."

"How are you using it?"

"I'm a cipher," she said, as if that was enough explanation. "I can mimic a signature to mask my non-existent one, slipping through the pauses in the reads."

"Whose signature are you using right now?" I asked, concerned. "Tell me it's not Hades or Persephone."

"Neither," she said, with the hint of a smile. "I'm mimicking Corbel's right now."

I shook my head. "Are you trying to get us killed?"

"Relax. He visits here regularly to make sure the apartment is fully stocked. Persephone can't use the space right now. They had some kind of break-in that destroyed half of the apartment."

I had heard about the break-in. My sources, by which I meant Frank and Cole, told me the destructive duo were involved somehow. It actually fit. The Eldorado was a landmark, and it was associated with Hades. Didn't take much more than that for those two. If it was true, I was surprised the building was still standing.

We got off on the top which was the only other floor this elevator stopped at. The hallway was covered in defensive runes that made anything I had about as strong as toilet paper.

"Proto-runes?" I asked, admiring the work. "This is some serious defense."

The only things I had that compared to this, were the runes in the duster and my photo-reactive ink. Both of those were done by mages more skilled and powerful than me.

"Hades did these himself," Koda said. "Even I can't read them. I just know they're old and powerful."

We walked down the hallway to the only door on the floor besides the elevator.

"I thought the North Tower was empty?"

"Originally it was for the water tower, but Hades installed a higher tech solution, something similar to an induction cooling system, and converted the top floor into the security apartment."

She placed her hand on the door and the lock clicked open. A deep bass sound accompanied by the smell of cinnamon, embraced me.

Inside, sitting on the sofa, was Corbel—the Hound of Hades.

"Do you two even realize you're being tracked?" he asked, as he tossed me something that resembled a super phone.

"What the hell is this?" I said, holding up the device. "More importantly, who is tracking us?"

"Division 13," Corbel said. "Did he give you a card?"

"Fuck me," I said under my breath. "Are you

serious?"

I handed him the card and looked daggers at Koda. Corbel crushed it, placed it in a small urn, and set it on fire. It took a surprisingly long time to burn.

"I taught you better than this. You have the digits?"

"Yes," she said sheepishly. "I'm sorry, Grey. SOP is to capture the information and destroy the original."

"You remember all those numbers?"

She nodded.

"Standard operating procedure, with the emphasis on *standard*, Koda," Corbel said, clearly upset. "Are you going soft? Getting so distracted with being a Night Warden that you're forgetting your training?"

"It was an oversight," she said. "It won't happen again."

"Oversights like that can get you killed. Both of you."

I didn't interrupt, because Corbel was right, but she wasn't his subordinate any longer.

"She got the message. Tell me how it works."

Koda remained silent at my side.

"The card is a special graphite polymer designed to read DNA impressions, once a current is run through the card."

"An electrical current?"

"A runically charged current, say, similar to one provided by a small dragon that works at a bar downtown."

"Shit, here I was, trying to use a secure line and—"

"It wouldn't have made a difference, because he already knows you're here."

"It's clever," I said. "No one suspects something like a business card. It's innocuous. Everyone uses them."

"I don't," Corbel said. "Neither do you."

"True," I said, holding up the device. "What's this for?"

"By now, you've figured something is going on at Ellis," Corbel said, pointing at the device. "That…is you two going to Ellis."

"I don't follow."

"That device gives off the same signal as the card. I turned it on the moment you stepped inside. You're going to make your call and inform Ronin and the Light Council of your plan to investigate Ellis Island."

"How did you—?" I started.

"Don't bother," Koda said. "There's a reason he's called the Hound of Hades."

I narrowed my eyes, and the realization hit.

"It was you," I said. "You were the reason the Archive saw her."

"Took you long enough," he said, nodding. "She was sloppy and deserved to be caught. I merely nudged their security systems."

"You tripped me up?" Koda hissed.

"I've been shadowstrutting the both of you for two days. Not once did either of you pick up on my presence."

"Two days?" Koda said. "Impossible."

"Let's see…" He pointed at me. "This one wants a warden bag, even though it will probably kill him. Neither of you can seem to keep that mage, Street, in one location."

"What are you talking about?"

"First, Haven, then FDR's armored car—nice Time Warp, by the way—now the Cloisters," Corbel said. "He won't remain there long either. He's too strong, even with the stasis and null room. He's somehow attracting the rummers and they will eventually find him. Even through the Cloisters' defenses."

"I think you'd better explain this shadowstrut to me," I said, my voice steel, keeping the fact that he gave off a distinct cinnamon smell to my senses, to myself. "It seems you *have* been around us for the last few days. I don't appreciate being spied on."

"This isn't a game, Grey," Corbel answered. "If she screws up, or Hades gets a whiff of the degradation of her skills, and I'm not just here to observe."

"What do you mean?" I asked, feeling the anger flow. "I told your boss, she stays with me, it's my rules. He doesn't get to decide to retire her."

"I can see you have plenty of experience dealing with gods," Corbel said, shaking his head. "You don't dictate rules to Hades. He lets you think you do. He's been moving you around the board like a pawn from the moment you accepted that dark blade."

I remained silent because I didn't trust myself to be civil. Then I decided being civil was overrated. I let the darkness inside slip out just a bit. Corbel took a step back.

"You tell your boss, we've got this situation under control."

"Do you? Really?"

"Yes...we do," I said, my words clipped.

"You forget I was there?"

"Meaning?"

"To date, you've encountered the Tenebrous twice. Once at Bethesda Terrace and once when you summoned it to you. Clever, by the way, using the coat and her leathers. Next time, I hope you don't let it kick your ass...again."

"It didn't kick my ass *this* time," I said. "And to date, I'm the only mage who faced it twice, and I'm still here to tell the tale."

"Sure, whatever you need to tell yourself, to sleep at night," he said. "I saw your dance with the tree. If it wasn't for the sword, you'd both be dead right now, or worse...controlled by your Fluffy."

"If you were there, why didn't you assist?"

"That's not how a shadowstrut works," Koda explained, her voice subdued. "It's an advanced skill used for reconnaissance and information gathering. It's like you're a ghost. Your energy signature is muted to almost nothing. Once in a shadowstrut, you can't engage or interact with the world the same way."

"I know some part of you sensed me, which is amazing in itself," he said, looking at me, then Koda. "But you should've been able to determine another presence was near you when I was."

"Thank you, I think," I said. "You heard everything?"

"No. Shadowstrutting didn't let me into Honor's office or your room, and I refused to get into that thing you call a vehicle. It's cursed and evil."

I took some solace in knowing he didn't overhear everything. This skill was a real threat. I took a deep breath to prevent myself from doing something rash, like shooting Corbel a few times, storming wherever Hades was currently, and burying Darkspirit in his scheming chest.

"Clearly, you're not doing this shadow-chacha now," I said with a growl. "Get your ass in gear and let's end this thing. If I make it through tonight, your boss and I are going to have words."

"That would be a bad idea, Grey. Seriously."

"You know what's a bad idea? Fucking with someone who has nothing to lose...*that* is a bad idea."

I grabbed the phone and dialed the digits. They weren't the only ones trained to use their memories.

THIRTY-FOUR

The call connected after a few rings and several seconds of silence.

I was sure it was being bounced all over and rerouted to disguise the origin point. I put the call on speaker.

"Grey," Ronin answered. "Good to hear you're still alive. I apologize for the inconvenience."

"Nearly getting me killed was an inconvenience?"

"You're a Night Warden, a real badass. Some mindless creatures posed you no real threat."

"About those coordinates you gave me—"

I needed to sell it.

"You deciphered it…good. Like I said, when you feel you can't trust anyone, I'm here for you."

"I appreciate it. I was calling to let you know we may have a lead."

"A lead? Are you sure? Maybe you should let me handle it. You have enough on your plate."

He was good. Reeling me in by trying to remove the prize. Classic psych move.

"We got it," I said, determined. "My apprentice and I will pop over to Ellis and do a quick search. There was some runic activity, but it was hard to pinpoint, due to the island being surrounded by moving water."

"That's why they call them islands," he said. "Are you heading over there now? What about the creature hunting the mages?"

"I think these may be related," I said. "We're still looking for the Redrum X supplier. I think he may be on this island."

"Are you going there alone?" he asked. "Do you need backup?"

"I have my apprentice," I said. "You know us Night Wardens, we work best alone."

"Got it," he said. "Let me know if I can be of assistance. I may not be with Division 13 officially, but I still have resources."

"Thanks, you've done enough. I'll reach out if I need an assist. Like I said, we're just going to do some recon, nothing major."

"Talk soon," he said. "Be safe out there."

I hung up the call.

"Are you going to be okay out there alone?" I asked Corbel, who headed for the door. "He's probably going to be bringing a large group of Light Council."

"I'll have my Tribus with me."

"Ouch," I said. "Try not to kill them. They're deluded and misinformed, not evil."

"They're threatening the wrong people." He glanced at Koda. "Some of the worst acts in history were committed by the deluded and misinformed. I will offer them an opportunity to leave with their lives. Whether they accept the offer—that's up to them."

"Corbel," I said, "don't kill them. If you do, I'll have to deal with a pissed-off Honor, and he's plenty pissed as it is. Hurt them, show them the error of their ways, just don't ghost them."

"Go stop the Tenebrous," he said. "I'll deal with Ronin and the Council. Lock up when you leave. Koda, remember: eyes and ears."

Corbel walked out.

"What did he mean, eyes and ears?" I asked. "Did he want you to finish...nose and mouth?"

"It's a Corbel thing. When we were training, he kept drilling us to use all of our senses. Eyes can miss things, and ears can hear incorrectly. We need to use all our senses to form a complete picture."

"Agreed," I answered. If I had paid attention to my sense of smell, I would have pinpointed that Corbel was doing his shadowstrut thing. "Good advice."

"Are you planning on facing the Tenebrous again?"

I nodded. "Kind of part of the job description. Face evil creatures bent on destroying others when everyone else is running away. You want to take a raincheck?"

Koda glared at me. "Excuse me?"

"I'd understand if you did."

"I'm not becoming a Night Warden to run from my fears."

I held up a hand in surrender. "I'm just saying. Getting body-checked by your fears can't be fun."

"Night Wardens have fun? I didn't get that memo. When does the fun start?"

"Tonight," I said. "I have a feeling Fluffy will be looking for Street."

"I thought the whole point of putting Street with Aria was to keep him safe?"

"That hasn't changed. Street will be safe."

"But you're using him as bait? Can you explain how that's keeping him safe?"

"He's not the bait, I am."

"You? You said Fluffy doesn't affect you. You don't get that whole 'fear' thing."

"No. Tonight, the part of unstable, deranged mage will be played by yours truly."

"That's not much of a stretch for you," Koda said. "You're going to make Fluffy think you're Street? It's met you. How do you plan on doing this?"

"I'm going to make it an offer it can't refuse."

THIRTY-FIVE

"It's too dangerous, Grey," Aria said, arms crossed, and she was shaking her head. "One miscalculation and it has you. Do you know how difficult it will be to kill a dark mage possessed by a Tenebrous?"

It was just the two of us in her office. She wore one of our Dive shirts that read: *If you find the food & drinks offensive-we suggest you stop finding us.*

This was matched with a pair of black jeans and combat boots. I wasn't used to seeing her out of her Wordweaver robes. Tonight, she was dressed for war. Holstered to one thigh, I saw a replica of Fatebringer. On her other leg, a thigh sheath held a blade covered in runes.

Her hair was pulled back in a tight braid that wee finished with several sharp hair clips and small daggers. It was like looking at Lara Croft's bigger, badder, kickass sister.

"Don't sound so broken up," I said, looking out the window of her office which was on the top level of the Cloisters. The sun would be dropping below the horizon in a few hours. "I'd hate to put you out."

"Melodrama doesn't suit you, Warden," Aria replied. "We're both pragmatists, you and I."

"True, and you know this is the best-case scenario."

"I don't want to *have* to kill you, Grey. This isn't a matter of *if* I can do it. Of course I can erase your ancient ass. I don't *want* to."

"I need to get the Tenebrous off the streets so I can focus on the Redrum X. This is the best way I can think of. If you have a better idea, I'm all ears."

"For the record, I'm livid you destroyed a duster to use it as fuel for a beacon. Do you know how much work goes into one of those coats?"

"I do."

I looked down at the empty grounds. Aria had had the Cloisters cleared out once I informed her my plan. We were going to bring Fluffy to us. In order to do that, we couldn't have targets of opportunity roaming the property for Fluffy to use. I wanted him to come for me, and me alone.

Only Aria, Koda, Street, and me were on the property. The fewer potential targets, the better. All of us had dealt with entities of power before, even though only Aria and I were doing the bulk of the damage. Koda would safeguard Street from any rummers that got past the defenses.

There weren't going to be many. We intended to open one side of the defenses and funnel them in. No matter how many rummers, rummogres, or other kinds of nastiness Fluffy created, the door into the Cloisters was going to be narrow. We'd create a kill-funnel. I would initially be outside the defenses, making my way back onto the property as Fluffy approached.

Being bait sucked.

With a little luck, Fluffy would follow me inside,

where we could trap and end it. I looked around the serene property again, realizing that by nightfall this entire area would be crawling with rummers and other assorted monsters.

The Wordweavers had taken ownership of the property from the Metropolitan Museum several decades back. They had kept the museum open but sealed off one side and the top floors for themselves.

The Cloisters contained architectural elements from four French medieval abbeys. What wasn't written in the tourism pamphlets was that these four abbeys were also ancient Wordweaver hubs of power. By combining these four elements, the site became a nexus of power.

Wordweavers have existed as long as magic. Some say they were the first magic-users. Haven was a medical facility with magical applications; The Cloisters were a magical facility with medical applications.

It also had one more function. With the right spells, the Cloisters served as a Wordweaver fortress. It had a sheer drop on one side, was situated on top of a mountain, and was next to the Hudson River. It was an ideal magical stronghold. Once closed, it was almost impossible to breach without being seen. Only the Night Warden's Shadow Helm compared to it, before it was leveled.

Aria sighed. "I don't have a better idea. Your plan is solid. We just haven't dealt with a creature like this in ages."

"I have the solution."

"A soulblaze? Do you understand what you're saying?"

"I do," I said. "It's one and done."

"Don't be glib," she said. "You're throwing your life away."

"No, no, I'm not. I've made peace with this, long before tonight."

"There has to be an alternative."

"Sure, and while we come up with it, how many more mages have to die?"

"Damn you, Grey."

"I care about you too, Aria. Thank you, for everything. I'd better go get ready."

THIRTY-SIX

"What the fuck?" Koda yelled. "You're going to do what? Hell no!"

We sat in the serene Cuxa Cloister at the heart of the property, the same way it would be in a monastery. Rose-pink marble columns, topped with carved capitals, surrounded the cloister garden with its central fountain and paths. The subtle thrum of power could be felt in every stone around us. It was an interesting contrast to Koda's raised voice and cursing.

"I've made arrangements for you," I said, trying to calm her down. "You're not going back to Hades."

"You think that's what I'm worried about?"

"Aren't you?"

"How dense can you possibly be? There are people who care about what happens to you… you…ass!"

So much for a calm conversation.

"You have a better idea?"

"Yes, any idea that doesn't involve you dying tonight. How about we start there?"

"Would love to, lay it on me."

"That's not fair, what you're doing. You think

you're being selfless, but really it's selfish. You haven't given any thought to how we feel. This is just the Night Warden's famous last stand."

"That's not what this is at all, and you know it."

"Do I? Have you exhausted every other option?"

"Yes, the only other way to deal with the Tenebrous is to erase whoever summoned it."

"Let's do that," she said, agitated. "I'm all for finding that fucker and ending him with extreme prejudice."

"In the meantime," I said, with a sigh, "how many more have to die while we look for the summoner?"

"What about Frank, Cole, and The Dive? Did you discuss this with Aria and Roxanne?"

"All of you will be taken care of," I said as gently as possible. "Aria and Cole are executors of my will."

"You still don't get it," Koda said, staring at me with wet eyes. "We don't want to be taken care of, you idiot. We don't want you to die. I don't want you to die."

She stomped off, leaving me alone. Or so I thought.

"Hello, Grey."

I turned to see Street sitting on the pink marble in between two columns. He was wearing a loose-fitting shirt and pants ensemble.

"Hello, Street."

"Seems like your apprentice is scared of losing you."

"I guess you could say that," I said, looking in the direction Koda had stomped off in. "She doesn't handle loss well."

Street nodded. "No one enjoys loss, really. Not of the things or people they hold dear."

"How are you?"

"Surprisingly lucid," he answered. "I'm guessing

sitting in a nexus of power, like this one, has beneficial effects for someone like me."

"Someone like you?"

"You know, slightly off, unstable, deranged, insane."

"Street—"

"Oh, no need to apologize," he said. "I'm well aware of my mental state when I'm this lucid, and therein lies the problem."

"What problem?"

"I'm losing what little mind I have left, Grey. The lapses are getting longer. I wake up in the middle of the park, not knowing how I got there. I'm wearing clothes I don't remember purchasing."

"We can get you—"

"Help?" Street laughed bitterly. "I'm a mage, Grey. I used to be part of a sect, accomplished and respected. Look at me. Do you know what a mage prizes above all else?"

I knew. "Yes."

"His mind," Street answered anyway, pointing to his temple. "A mage's mind is his greatest possession, and I'm losing mine."

He held his hands out in front of him, and I could see the tremors. He grabbed one hand with the other, lowering them and resting them on his lap.

"Maybe you can stay here? I'm sure Aria can make arrangements to keep you here."

Street shook his head slowly. "You know me. I'll be here a few weeks, and then the wanderlust sets in. I'll leave the property and my sanity behind. Then that thing will find me. I don't want to end things like that, as some creature's plaything, slowly dying. What if it makes me hurt someone? Kill someone?"

"We won't…it won't…it doesn't have to end at all," I stumbled. "We're going to stop it, tonight."

"I'm going out on my own terms, Grey."

"What are you talking about? You're not going out on any terms. I'll speak to Aria."

"Thank you, Grey, for everything," Street said, with a sad smile, "especially the shoes and the food. I won't ever forget that."

He started walking away, heading to the interior.

"You have plenty of shoes and food in your future, Street," I called out after him. "You make sure you stay inside with Koda when it begins. Understand?"

He nodded, waved a hand, and turned a corner as the sun dropped behind the horizon, ending the day.

"I should just change my name to Grey Stryder, Morale Booster," I muttered to myself. I was about to get Koda to stick to Street, when Aria's voice came over my comms.

"Grey, we have incoming," she said. "I'll get Street covered, and you initiate the plan. We rendezvous in the garden."

"You heard that...Koda?"

"I'm on it," Koda said, in her clipped voice. "I'll meet with her and take Street to the secure location."

I ran to the entrance.

THIRTY-SEVEN

My carefully well-thought-out plan lasted exactly twenty seconds of contact with the enemy. To be fair, I never counted on the trollgres.

"What do you mean we have incoming?" I asked as I ran to the pre-planned breach. "I didn't light the beacon."

"What part of that statement is unclear? Rummers are advancing on the property in organized phalanxes. This is like a scene out of a Peter Jackson movie. Except we are not standing opposite Mordor. I've never seen rummers act in a coordinated manner, ever."

"Fluffy is controlling them."

"What the fresh hell is that?"

I heard the crash, the foghorn of death, and tasted bitter lemon in my mouth all at once.

"Shit, what was that?" I said. "Aria, status?"

"I don't know what I'm looking at, and I've seen some strange creatures in my time," she said. "This looks like someone mashed together a troll with an ogre. Both ugly creatures producing an uglier combination. This is not a pretty mix."

"A Trollgre? Fluffy isn't fooling around."

Another crash and a roar.

"There's another one of those troll-ogre things on the south wall," she said, and I heard gunfire. "At this rate, they'll break through the defenses, Grey. I do hope you have a Plan B."

"I do," I said, moving back to the center of the Cloisters. "Koda, you keep Street safe. Aria, you and I erase everything else."

"That sounds very similar to Plan A," Aria shot back. "You'd better attract the Tenebrous to your position. I have more than my fair share of rummers to deal with."

I formed Darkspirit and unleashed the darkness.

<Finally, mage. Yes.>

Black tendrils of power raced around my arm and Darkspirit.

I smelled chlorine and heard the thunderclap. This wasn't the usual Frank thunderclap. A bolt of energy struck the ground nearby, nearly blinding me, followed by several more striking all around the property.

"Grey? What are you doing, trying to destroy the building?"

"It's backup," I said, looking down with a smile at the bright, glowing pink thorny dragon. "Frank brought friends."

"One word about the color and I feed you to those monsters on the walls."

"What color?" I said, bringing a hand to my ear. "I think I'm hearing the voice of that rare species—the Fuchsia Dragon."

"Hilarious," Frank snapped. "I could feed you to the creatures redecorating the walls."

"By the way, who are all these people?"

"Mages, most of them from the street. Somehow

they've heard that you and the Night Wardens might need help tonight."

"There's so many of them," I said, looking at the mages attacking the rummers and then I realized how bad this had just become. "Frank! They need to keep away from Fluffy. He'll use their fears against them and us. Tell them!"

Frank disappeared in a flash of light as I dodged an orb of red energy. I sliced through rummers, converting them to dust as they raced at me. In the distance, I saw what I was looking for: A lone figure standing back from the fighting, surrounded by three trollgres.

Hideous didn't begin to describe them. They weren't as large as actual trolls, but they easily outclassed the rummogres. Judging from the blasts that hit them and yet did no damage, they were immune to most magic. They were fast, and they used their massive fists and legs with frightening precision.

Nothing and no one was getting past them. If I was going to take down Fluffy, I needed to get past the bodyguards to use the soulblaze effectively.

I ran at the figure who was currently facing away from me. As I stepped closer, I realized Fluffy had chosen a female host this time.

When she turned, I looked into the face of my old partner, the woman I loved, the woman I killed.

It was Jade.

THIRTY-EIGHT

I never saw the fist coming.

Frank blasted me and tried to shove me sideways out of its path. He was partially successful. The fist caught me in a glancing blow and bounced me off a wall. Everywhere around me, the Cloisters were a battleground. I was disoriented as the trollgre came in for the killing blow. Another mage, someone I never knew, shoved me out of the way and took a bone-shattering kick to the back.

I saw the life leave his eyes as he crumpled to the ground, and I woke up.

<End them, Izanami.>

<With pleasure.>

Blackness exploded around me as the anger flared in my chest. The tendrils consumed the rummers that were brave or stupid enough to get close. Trollgre One, who had kicked the life out of the mage, grinned at me, outstretching his arms, daring me to approach. I took his invitation and sprinted. In half a second, I had buried Darkspirit in his eye. A roar filled the garden.

I removed the sword from his face and slashed horizontally, separating head from body, before it burst into dust. The sudden silence was deafening. More rummers leaped at me. I unleashed dozens of orbs, obliterating rummers where they stood.

Dark energy flowed through me as I approached Trollgre Two.

This one was smarter and stayed away from Darkspirit. It circled around as I focused on it.

<Move, mage.>

I dropped to the ground, avoiding a haymaker from Trollgre Three, who had tried to flank me. I rolled to the side and away from a life-stopping stomp from Trollgre Two. Trollgre Three launched a handful of rummers at me. I stood my ground and sliced through them, realizing my mistake too late. As soon as I finished my slash, Trollgre Two introduced me to his massive fist.

This time I caught the full impact on my side and felt something break, probably a rib or two. My duster dissipated most of the blow as I sailed across the garden. I landed on my back and slid into one of the marble walls. I felt the tremors as the trollgre closed in on me.

<Next time, maybe tell me which direction?>

<You have a creature fast approaching. Stop limiting me and let me deal with these vermin.>

<That's precisely why I won't.>

I slid to the side and jumped through a pair of columns as a bolt of energy sliced through the air, incinerating Trollgre Two.

"A little warning next time?"

"You're welcome," Frank yelled. "Watch it!"

I turned and parried several orbs that exploded on contact, wrenching Darkspirit from my grip. The sword sailed across the garden and over a wall. I extended an arm, but nothing. The runic defenses must have interrupted my absorption ability.

I drew Fatebringer and dropped several rummers, but their numbers seemed endless. I ran to where I thought Darkspirit had landed and felt a tug on my duster. Trollgre Three yanked me back by my coat, nearly giving me whiplash. The fact that the duster didn't tear or rip was a testament to the craftsmanship of the Wordweavers. It also meant I was heading into the waiting arms of an angry Trollgre who was going to hug me into oblivion.

I fired Fatebringer two more times. The rounds were a distraction, but they bought me enough time to cast. I whispered the spell and unleashed death, as pain grabbed me by the temples. One of my eyes stopped working as the excruciating pain blinded me. I stumbled back just in time to see Trollgre Three be consumed by black eldritch flame. It screamed and tore at itself as the flames burned.

More rummers advanced, and I realized, in that moment, we were probably all going to die. I had come to terms with it, I just wanted to make sure I ghosted Fluffy first.

"Grey!" Koda yelled in the comms. "Street is gone."

THIRTY-NINE

Out of the corner of my one functioning eye, I saw Street.

He had found Darkspirit, and he was advancing on Fluffy. It was exactly what the Tenebrous wanted. If Street got close enough, it could take over his body and use him as the perfect host.

"Street! No!" I yelled. "Stay away from it!"

Street closed the distance and thrust forward. Fluffy opened its arms and let him impale the body it was using. Street removed Darkspirit and was about to attempt a second thrust, when Fluffy grabbed him and spun Street around to face me, preventing a second thrust.

"Shit." I ran over to them and realized I was too late. "Street, what have you done?"

Fluffy howled with laughter as he merged with Street. I saw the tendrils of energy envelop the both of them. In moments, Street would be gone, and the Tenebrous would have the perfect host.

Street lifted the sword and threw it at me. I caught Darkspirit, and power surged in my body.

"Do it, Grey," Street rasped. "Use me for the soulblaze."

Fluffy's eyes opened wide when he realized what Street had said.

"Street, no," I said. "It will kill you."

"You idiot! What do you think is going to happen if you let this finish? Let me go out my way. Cast the soulblaze."

"Grey, no," pleaded Fluffy in Jade's voice. "Please, we can be together now. Please don't kill me. We can have the life you've always wanted, away from the patrols. You can stop being a Warden, and we can live a life of peace. Please, Grey."

"Do it, Warden," Street said with the last of his strength, as his body sagged forward. "Do it now!"

I cast the soulblaze, using Street as the focus. The garden erupted in bright yellow light as the creatures around us were consumed.

"The sword, Grey!" Frank yelled. "Use the sword!"

I thrust forward and drove Darkspirit through Street and Fluffy. The power raced into me, shredding the duster as it blew through my body. I held on for the longest ten seconds of my life.

When it was done, Street fell forward, and Koda caught him. Fluffy fell to its knees. I could see it was done.

"Why didn't it work?" Fluffy said. "I offered you the one thing you wanted. I saw it in your mind."

"You may have seen it, but Jade would've never wanted me to stop being a Warden. You lose. Now get the hell out of here."

"You may have destroyed me, but I have given you fear. You fear losing those closest to you. I have won."

"You didn't win," I said, looking around at the battered, beaten, and bruised faces of my friends—my family. "You didn't give me fear. Tonight, I faced that fear and beat it, beat you. Tonight, I claimed my family."

The Tenebrous burst into a cloud of dust, vanishing in the gentle wind.

FORTY

TWO DAYS LATER—CLOISTERS

"Y ou played me, Ronin," I said, holding the phone
gingerly against my still aching head.

"Don't take it personally, Grey. Besides, I needed
to test the defenses at the Central Archive."

"So, you used me as your mule."

"You were already burned with them. It made
perfect sense."

"You are a total piece of shit, Ronin. Honor is
okay, by the way."

"Don't get this twisted, Grey. It's not about you or
a group of homeless mages. There's a group out there
that wants to destroy—everything."

"Tigris kicking your ass?"

"Where did you hear that name?" Ronin said.
Suddenly I had his attention. "What do you know
about them?"

"Nothing. I'm just a lowly Night Warden, roaming
the streets and keeping those homeless mages from
being preyed on—you know, the insignificant stuff."

"Fuck you, Grey," Ronin said, his voice low and
seasoned with a deep-seated anger. "This is what

217

doomed the Night Wardens from the start. Your vision is myopic. You worry about the homeless mages, when the city's at stake. The city, when the country is in danger. The country, when it's the world. The Night Wardens were a mistake from their inception."

"I can see you've given this some thought, but I've learned a few things in the past few days too," I said, keeping my voice calm. "You can't take yourself too seriously—an old lady taught me that—and you honor those who stand with you when it all goes to shite."

"Wonderful. Life lessons from a washed up, has-been Warden. Thank you, now my life is complete."

"I learned something else, Ronin. I learned that someone has to speak for the voiceless. For the ones who will be slaughtered while the world turns a blind eye. That's what the Night Wardens are for. When everyone runs away, we run towards."

"Is that it?" Ronin asked. "You called to hit me with some antiquated Warden sayings? Give me a break. The Light Council is going to retire you and your apprentice. Good riddance to bad rubbish. Anything else?"

"I'll be seeing you soon, Ronin."

"Not if I see you first."

I hung up.

I understood the mentality. Ronin wasn't a bad operative, and he certainly wasn't a dark mage. Not that I was one to make a judgment call. He was simply misinformed and was touting the Division-13 line. I would take some time in the future to take him on a patrol and educate him about his world view. It was all in the details.

"You have a guest," Aria said, stepping into my room. "You up for it?"

"Is it Roxanne? Because I don't think I can do another session of 'I told you so' from her."

I heard the wind chimes and smelled the strong coffee.

I sat up and motioned for Aria to let my guest in.

"Hello, Grey."

She was dressed in her usual black-on-black. The power coming off her was impressive, especially considering I was lying in the strongest null room in the Cloisters.

"Thank you for coming," I said. "You didn't have to come all this way."

"Dex informed me you were looking for one of these." She patted the bundle on her side. "These are rare, and the cost is high. Are you sure you're willing to pay it?"

"It could have made my last encounter with a Tenebrous slightly easier."

"Or it could have killed everyone. Hard to see how these things go sometimes."

"True. I'm willing to pay the cost."

"We will see."

She placed the bundle next to me on the bed and stepped back.

"Thank you again."

"Once you've recovered sufficiently, I expect to see you and"—she glanced over to the corner—"your apprentice at the Boutique."

"Of course."

"Oh, and Warden?" she said as she gestured.

"Yes?"

"Don't make me come looking for you. That would be an unpleasant experience—for you."

"Wouldn't even consider it."

"Excellent. I *will* see you soon, then."

A portal opened next to her, and she disappeared.

"Stop hiding...she's gone."

"Was that her?" Koda asked. "She's fierce."

"More like fearsome, but fierce fits too."

"When are we going to visit her?"

"As soon as I can get dressed," I said. "I'm not about to risk pissing off TK."

"That would be prudent," Aria said from the door. "Even I would hesitate to engage her or her husband in combat."

"Thank you again, for everything."

"Before you go,"—Aria gestured—"I wanted to make sure you were both dressed accordingly."

Two dusters materialized on the bed. Well, one was a duster, the other was duster-like, complete with hood, for a certain cipher.

"Is that one for me?" Koda asked, her voice filled with awe. "Are you serious?"

"I'd say you earned it, and Grey agrees."

"No more Night Warden in training," I said. "Well, you still have plenty of training to go through, and your attitude leaves much to be desired, not to mention—"

"Grey?" Aria said. "The words you're looking for are: Congratulations, Night Warden Koda."

"Right. Congratulations, Night Warden Koda."

THE END

***

Author Notes

Thank you for reading this story and jumping back into a world of Grey and the Night Wardens. Writing this story was both exciting and bittersweet. Anytime a character dies in one of my books it impacts me. I can't help thinking that maybe, just maybe I can save the character. This time there was no way around it, really. Writing the Night Warden books and Grey in particular, requires a darker frame of mind. Grey is a broken man living in a broken world, trying to do good. Even if it kills him. Through it all, he manages to keep his dark sense of humor, even though he leans somewhat on the cynical side. He has good friends, and a smartass apprentice that keep him mostly sane and well-caffeinated.

Thank you for stepping into Grey's (and Koda's) world and sharing a few hours of your time with me.

My main series, Montague & Strong has produced several tangent stories, each with rich and exciting characters. This series is a direct tangent to Monty & Simon's adventures and you will hear them, or their exploits mentioned regularly in the Night Warden novels. Occasionally they will make cameo appearances, although Grey isn't keen about Simon and his devildog dropping by The Dive. The danger of destruction and devastation is too great, plus he doesn't keep that many sausages in stock.

The influences in my writing were (and are) many, but the goal is still the same. Write a good story. Create a character you'd want to spend some time with, and join them as they deal with situations that spiral out of control as a result of the actions and choices. For me, that's the recipe for a book that immerses me in the story, and makes it hard to put down.

It's my sincere wish that I achieved a small measure of that with SHADOWSTRUT.

I want to thank you again for reading this story. If you would like a different story with a dose of magic, snark, sausages, and destruction, I'd like to suggest

221

my Montague & Strong series. It's the ongoing story of an immortal detective, an ever-hungry hellhound companion, and an angry mage working the cases only they can.

A reminder: if you really enjoyed this story, please take a few moments and **kindly leave a review** at the site you purchased it from. It doesn't have to be long…just a line or two would be fantastic and it would really help me out.

SPECIAL MENTIONS

Tammy of the WOUF: who imagined, designed and created the Warden Bag. Thank you Tammy.

For the special boots created for Koda after you broke your toe and renamed the post-op boot, Dead Sexy. Because of course it would be named that.

For snarkasm and other assorted additions to the english language …I will be calling Merriam-Webster soon.

Davina for the immense amount of commas and the GOT nod…not today. I apologize for making you unleash the Tao of Comma on this book.

For the Billy Goats Gruff reference for tastier light mages lol.

Orlando A. Sanchez
www.orlandoasanchez.com

Orlando has been writing ever since his teens when he was immersed in creating scenarios for playing Dungeon and Dragons with his friends every weekend. The worlds of his books are urban settings with a twist of the paranormal lurking just behind the scenes and generous doses of magic, martial arts, and mayhem. He currently resides in Queens, NY with his wife and children and can often be found lurking in the local coffee shops where most of his writing is done.

BITTEN PEACHES PUBLISHING

Thanks for Reading
If you enjoyed this book, would you please **leave a review** at the site you purchased it from? It doesn't have to be long... just a line or two would be fantastic and it would really help me out.

Bitten Peaches Publishing offers more books by this author. From science fiction & fantasy to adventure & mystery, we bring the best stories for adults and kids alike.

www.BittenPeachesPublishing.com

More books by Orlando A. Sanchez

The Warriors of the Way
The Karashihan*•The Spiritual Warriors•The Ascendants•The Fallen Warrior•The Warrior Ascendant•TheMaster Warrior

John Kane
The Deepest Cut*•Blur

BITTEN PEACHES PUBLISHING

Sepia Blue
The Last Dance*•Rise of the
Night•Sisters•Nightmare

Chronicles of the Modern Mystics
The Dark Flame•A Dream of Ashes

Montague & Strong Detective Agency Novels
Tombyards & Butterflies•Full Moon Howl•Blood is
Thicker•Silver Clouds Dirty
Sky•Homecoming•Dragons & Demigods•Bullets &
Blades•Hell Hath No Fury

Montague & Strong Detective Agency Stories
No God is Safe•The Date•The War Mage•A Proper
Hellhound

Brew & Chew Adventures
Hellhound Blues

Night Warden Novels
Wander•ShadowStrut

Division 13
The Operative•The Magekiller

Blackjack Chronicles
The Dread Warlock

The Assassins Apprentice
The Birth of Death

*Books denoted with an asterisk are **FREE** via my
website—www.orlandoasanchez.com

ACKNOWLEDEGEMENTS

With each book, I realize that every time I learn something about this craft, it highlights so many things I still have to learn. Each book, each creative expression, has a large group of people behind it.

This book is no different.

Even though you see one name on the cover, it is with the knowledge that I am standing on the shoulders of the literary giants that informed my youth and supported by my generous readers who give of their time to jump into the adventures of my overactive imagination.

I would like to take a moment to express my most sincere thanks:

To my Tribe: You are the reason I have stories to tell. You cannot possibly fathom how much and how deeply I love you all.

To Lee: Because you were the first audience I ever had. I love you sis.

To the Logsdon Family: The words, *Thank You* are

insufficient to describe the gratitude in my heart for each of you. JL your support always demands I bring my best, my A-game, and produce the best story I can. Both you and Lorelei(my Uber Jeditor) are the reason I am where I am today. Thank you for the notes, challenges, corrections, advice, and laughter. Your patience is truly infinite. *Arigatogozaimasu.*

To The Montague & Strong Case Files Group-AKA The MoB (Mages of Badassery): When I wrote T&B there were fifty-five members in The MoB. As of this release there are over one-thousand members in the MoB. I am honored to be able to call you my MoB Family. Thank you for being part of this group and M&S. You make this possible. **THANK YOU.**

To the WTA-The Incorrigibles: JL, Ben Z. Eric QK. S.S.

They sound like a bunch of badass misfits, because they are. My exposure to the deranged and deviant brain trust you all represent helped me be the author I am today. I have officially gone to the *dark side* thanks to all of you. I humbly give you my thanks, and…it's all your fault.

To the The English Advisory: Aaron, Penny, Carrie and all of the UK MoB. For all things English…thank you.

To DEATH WISH COFFEE: This book (and every book I write) has been fueled by generous amounts of the only coffee on the planet (and in space, yes, really, look it up) strong enough to power my very twisted imagination. Is there any other coffee that can compare? I think not. DEATH WISH-Thank you!

To the Gene Mollica Studio: Gene, Sasha, and the crew.

Your covers can only be described as ART. Thank you for taking the time to create the masterpieces you do. Readers always want your covers as memorabilia because they look like movie posters. You never fail to amaze me with your professionalism, talent, skill, and creativity. Thank you for the great service and amazing covers!

To you the reader: I was always taught to save the best for last. I write these stories for you. Thank you for jumping down the rabbit holes of *what if?* with me. You are the reason I write the stories I do. You keep reading…I'll keep writing.

Thank you for your support and encouragement.

CONTACT ME

I really do appreciate your feedback. You can let me know what you thought of the story by emailing me at:

www.orlando@orlandoasanchez.com

To get **FREE** stories please visit my page at:
www.orlandoasanchez.com

For more information on Grey & Koda...come join the MoB Family on Facebook!
You can find us at:
Montague & Strong Case Files

If you enjoyed the book, please leave a review HERE. They really help the book and other readers find good stories to read. THANK YOU!

ART SHREDDERS

No book is the work of one person. I am fortunate enough to have an amazing team of advance readers and shredders. They give their time and keen eyes to provide notes, insight, and corrections (dealing wonderfully with my dreaded comma allergy). They help make every book and story go from good to great. Each and every one of you helped make this book fantastic.

THANK YOU

<u>ART SHREDDERS</u>

Adam G. Alex P. Amanda H. Amy R. Anne M. Audrey C. Barbara H. Barbara H. Bennah P. Beverly C. Carrie Anne O'L. Cassandra H. Chris C II. Corinne L. Dana A. Daniel P. Darren M. Davina N. Denise K. Diane K. Dolly S. Dorothy MPG. Hal B. Helen G. Helen D. Jan G. Jen C. Jim S. Joscelyn S. Julie P. Karen H. Karen H. Kirsten B.W. Larry D. T. Laura C. R. Laura T. Lesley S. Mary Anne P. Melissa M. Melody D. Mike H. Natalie F. Patricia O'N. RC B. Rene' C.

ART SHREDDERS

Rob H. Sara M.B. Shannon O.B. Sharon H. Stacey S.
Stephanie C. Stephen B. Steve W. Tami C. Tammy T.
Tanya A. Terri A. Thomas R. Wendy S.

Thanks for Reading
If you enjoyed this book, would you please leave a review at the site you purchased it from? It doesn't have to be a book report... just a line or two would be fantastic and it would really help us out!

Made in the USA
Monee, IL
29 April 2024

57670715R00142